the casket and the sword

the casket and the sword

by NORMAN DALE

Pictures by Irv Docktor

HARPER & BROTHERS
PUBLISHERS
NEW YORK

THE CASKET AND THE SWORD

Printed in the United States of America

First Edition

1–F

Library of Congress catalog card number: 56–10367

contents

the casket and the sword

CHAPTER 1

the trumpet call

JEREMY HAD HAD MEASLES RATHER BADLY, and the doctor said that he needed a change of air before going back to school. Jeremy was delighted, hoping that this would mean an unexpected visit to the seaside. But it happened in June, in the middle of the summer term, and the family were not having their holiday until August. They had no friends or relations living at the seaside. The only thing to do with Jeremy was to send him to stay for a fortnight with Aunt Eleanor, who lived by herself in a cottage near a village in the West Country. He was not sure, at first, whether he liked this idea or not.

Aunt Eleanor was tall and thin with a sharp, peaky face and dark hair that was generally untidy. She wore unusual, gay-looking clothes, but Jeremy's mother said she was very careless about them. "If only Eleanor would take more trouble with herself," Mother said, "she'd be very good-looking. But if she will bury herself in the middle of nowhere with her painting, how can she ever expect to get married?" Jeremy did not see why Aunt Eleanor should get married if she didn't want to, or why she shouldn't paint pictures if that was what she liked doing (and she did it extremely well). On the whole he was on her side, but he did not feel that he had ever really got to know her.

She was a person who did and said unexpected things. As a rule when she came to stay with Jeremy's family in London she did not take much notice of Jeremy and his two sisters, Elizabeth and Ann, who were aged nine and six (Jeremy was nearly thirteen). But sometimes she would surprise them by going for a walk or joining in a game, and sometimes she would sit and make sketches of them in the garden. This bothered them at first, because they thought they were supposed to keep still; but she said in her sharp-sounding way:

"For Heaven's sake don't stand about looking stuffed! Just do whatever you want, and don't take any notice of me."

It was not easy to take no notice of her as she sat watching them with quick, dark eyes while her hand moved rapidly over the sketch-book on her knee. But they soon discovered that she was not a person to be shy of, however sharp she sounded. She looked quite different when she smiled. She also had a way of producing chocolates at unexpected moments, and (which was surprising) she generally remembered birthdays.

But still she was strange to them. The only time Jeremy had had a real conversation with her was one afternoon when she came to the end of the garden with her sketch-book, and found him trying to play a tin whistle someone had given him. It was just an ordinary whistle with six holes, and since no one had taught him how to play it Jeremy was getting nothing out of it except squeaks. He stopped as soon as Aunt Eleanor appeared, and she said:

"Here, give that thing to me."

She took it from him and played a scale. Then she played "Pop Goes the Weasel," "D'ye ken John Peel?" and "There Is a Green Hill Far Away" without making a single mistake.

"Gosh!" said Jeremy.

"Now watch," said Aunt Eleanor. "This is how it's done."

The way you play a tin whistle is this. First you cover all six holes and blow. You have to blow steadily, not too hard or soft, controlling your breath. This gives you the lowest note of the scale. Then you uncover the bottom hole, and this gives you the next note. Then you uncover two holes, then three, and so on until you have uncovered all six. You have now played seven notes of the scale. In order to get the eighth note you have to cover all the holes except the top one, the one nearest the mouthpiece.

Once you have learned to play a scale you can start practicing tunes. A good one to begin on is "Home, Sweet Home," because this is all in one octave and contains no sharps or flats. You get these by half covering a hole, which makes them more difficult. You can also get the higher octave by simply blowing harder; but it must be said that the higher you go on a tin whistle the more piercing its note becomes, and people don't always like it very much.

While Jeremy practiced the scale Aunt Eleanor sat sketching and making occasional remarks. Presently she asked:

"What's your favorite subject at school?"

"History," said Jeremy.

He could answer the question without thinking because he was used to it. As a rule when he told them people said "History, eh? Ah. H'm" and then went on to talk about something else. But Aunt Eleanor surprised him by giving him a quick glance and saying:

"Why?"

"Well, I'm generally top in it," said Jeremy, wrinkling his forehead.

She laughed.

"You like it because you're top in it, and you're top in it because you like it! It was a silly question anyway. But history was always my favorite subject, too, although I doubt if I was ever top in it—no good at dates!"

Jeremy thawed out at this. Aunt Eleanor looked much younger when she smiled.

"I like math as well," he said. "But history—well, it's a story. And it's true. It all happened."

"And still does," said Aunt Eleanor. "It's a story that goes on and on. I used to think of it as something far off and romantic, but that was just schoolgirlish. Now I like it for the opposite reason—because it's so close to us."

"One doesn't seem to notice it much," said Jeremy, wrinkling his forehead again.

"You do if you look. And sometimes you're made to realize it in unexpected and exciting ways. History's all round us. It's what we are. It's part of the things we do, and even of the things we think. We're like the leaves on a tree. We shouldn't be anywhere without the roots."

The conversation died away. Jeremy played a few more scales and then, at Aunt Eleanor's suggestion, he tried "Home, Sweet Home." After several attempts he managed to play the first part well enough for the tune to be recognized.

"You're getting the hang of it rather quickly," said Aunt Eleanor. "You must have a good ear for music."

Jeremy was extraordinarily pleased. It was a thing he had always wanted to be able to do—to play tunes on an instrument of some kind. He had tried hard with a mouth-organ but had found it too difficult. And now he knew that it could be done. He had only to go on practicing with his whistle and he would be able to play any number of tunes.

He went on practicing while Aunt Eleanor went on drawing, taking no notice of the squeaks and wrong notes. She had torn a sheet off her pad and started something else. At last she tore this off too, got to her feet, and tossed it to him with a smile.

"There's a present for you," she said, and strolled back into the house.

Jeremy examined it with great interest. Aunt Eleanor

was a well-known painter, and her pictures were hung in galleries. It was a drawing of three boys. The first wore doublet and hose and had a lute in his hand. The second wore knee breeches and a long, open jacket with a waistcoat, and he was holding a violin. The third wore shorts and was sitting on the grass with a whistle to his lips. But they all had Jeremy's face and shock of untidy fair hair.

He sat poring over it and smiling as he thought of their conversation; and presently he went indoors and put the drawing carefully away in the box where he kept the things he valued most.

This had happened on a fine afternoon in March. Aunt Eleanor had left London the next day, and Jeremy had not seen her since. But he had remembered her. She was different from other people. He had a queerly excited feeling as he sat in the train on the long journey from Paddington. It was his first visit to the West Country and the first time, as a matter of fact, that he had ever been on a journey by himself. And of course it was rather fun to be doing something like this in mid-term, when everyone else was at school, even if it did mean missing cricket. But these were not the only reasons for his excitement. When Mother had put him on the train she had been full of last-minute warnings about remembering his manners, combing his hair, not sniffing, and wiping his shoes on the mat—all quite right, of course, and one would have to do one's best. But as the train pulled out of the station Jeremy had a feeling that he was leaving all those things behind. The thought of Aunt Eleanor made him feel that he was going into a different sort of world.

When at last he got out at the small country station Aunt Eleanor came striding down the platform to meet him, wearing green velvet slacks and a red-and-white check shirt, with her dark hair blowing in the breeze. Jeremy went toward her lugging his suitcase, which was rather heavy because in addition to his clothes it contained several books for reading on wet days. It also contained his whistle, on which he could now play seven tunes, including "God Save the Queen" and "Auld Lang Syne."

Aunt Eleanor took the case from him.

"Let's have a look at you, Jeremy. Rather washed out! Was the measles horrid?"

"Only while my throat was sore," said Jeremy. "After that it wasn't so bad."

"Well, I've got to try to fatten you up—lots of chicken and eggs and cream and honey! But the first thing is to get you home as quick as we can. I brought the trap because it's so much nicer than the car, but now it looks as though it's going to rain. We've five miles to go, and Biddy doesn't at all like hurrying."

Biddy was a small, plump mare waiting for them between the shafts of a pony trap such as one does not often see on the roads nowadays. Jeremy, who had never been in one before, rather enjoyed it. It was open and quiet, and you could talk comfortably as you jogged along and looked about you. The country was fairly flat at first, but presently it became hilly, some of the hills being so steep that Aunt Eleanor got out and walked beside the trap, still holding the reins. They passed through one small village, and saw a few scattered farmhouses and cottages.

"It's a bit lonely, isn't it?" said Jeremy, thinking of the streets of London.

"It's out of the world, certainly, but I don't find it lonely. There's plenty of life going on in fields and trees and hedges, if you use your eyes. There are plenty of people, too—near enough to be handy when you want them, but not so near that you have to be always seeing them. That's what I prefer."

"Have you been here long?"

"Only about eighteen months. I came here because—well, for various reasons. It's a good place to paint in."

"Your cottage is in a village, isn't it?"

"Just a little way outside. We shall be there in a few minutes." Aunt Eleanor glanced at him. "Are you feeling tired?"

"A bit," said Jeremy. "On account of the measles, I suppose. But it's awfully nice."

He said this out of politeness, without being quite sure if it was what he really thought. The countryside was certainly pretty, but it seemed a little dull.

However, a minute later he saw something to arouse his interest. They had turned off the road down a narrow lane with high hedges, which went steeply downhill until it emerged into a valley and ran beside a river. On the far side of the river was a footpath, beyond which was a very high brick wall, quite unlike the low stone walls that were common in those parts. There seemed to be no end to this wall, which curved away out of sight in either direction. Beyond it Jeremy could see nothing but steeply rising ground entirely covered by trees.

"What's that place?" he asked.

"It's an estate called Castlecombe, but the local people just call it the Old Park. And it belongs to Lord Castlecombe, who's known as the Old Earl." Aunt Eleanor glanced at Jeremy. "Have you ever heard of Castlecombe?"

"No, I don't think so," said Jeremy. "Why?"

"I thought you might have. Our family—that's to say, your father's family—used to live in these parts. But it was a long time ago, and there's no particular reason why you should have heard about it. Anyway, the Old Earl isn't there now. He used to be very rich, but he lost nearly all his money and went abroad, and now I believe the place is up for sale. There's a simply enormous old house, but it's right in the middle of the Park, with woods all round it, so that you can't see it at all from outside. It's empty now except for a caretaker and his wife, and a few men to look after the animals."

"What animals?" asked Jeremy.

"Cattle and deer mostly, I think, although there used to be all kinds. The Old Earl collected wild animals, you see. He had a private menagerie. Some were in cages, but the ones that weren't too wild were allowed to run loose in the Park. That's why he built the wall."

"Do you mean he had lions and tigers and—"

"I don't know," said Aunt Eleanor, smiling. "If he had, they must all have been sold by now. I can't tell you very much about it because I've never been inside. The Park was closed when the Old Earl went away, before I came to live here. But in the old days people used to pay a shilling to go in, on one or two afternoons a week, and then there were all kinds of exciting creatures running wild—strange foreign breeds of sheep and cattle, and all kinds of deer and antelope, and even kangaroos, I believe, and monkeys, and llamas from Peru. And peacocks on the lawns. There's an artificial lake which had all kinds of water birds on it. It must have been wonderful then!"

"And now you can't even go in!" said Jeremy in great disappointment.

"No. The gates are always locked, and there are dogs to chase the village boys if they climb over the wall. But the truth is, I don't think people much want to go there now."

"Why not?"

"Because it's so changed, I suppose. A great place like that becomes very sad and lonely when it isn't lived in as it should be—and perhaps a little frightening, too. It's old, you see; it's very old."

Aunt Eleanor then suddenly changed the subject in a way which made Jeremy feel that she did not want to go on talking about the Old Park.

"Did I tell you that there's a fair at Reddicombe next week?" she asked abruptly. "Swings and merry-go-rounds, and everything! I hope you like fairs. We shall have to try and win some prizes!"

A moment later the road left the river, curving round to climb through a gap between two low hills. And just beyond this ridge, on an expanse of flat, open land, was Aunt Eleanor's cottage.

Although the cottage itself was small, it had a big garden and a paddock of about three acres, where Biddy grazed, sharing it with a lot of chickens. There was also a stable and a garage, and at the end of the garden a small separate building with a big skylight in its slate roof. This was Aunt Eleanor's studio.

Jeremy had only a glimpse of it all when they arrived, because the rain was just starting. Aunt Eleanor drove in at the open gates and pulled up at the front door, calling:

"Jonas, where are you? Come and take Biddy!"

A bent old man came hobbling toward them from behind a hedge.

"Here I be!" he said in a grumbling voice. "There weren't no need to shout. I heerd 'ee!"

At the same time the door was opened by a plump, gray-haired woman with a round red face.

"So you got back in time," she said. "But only just! It'll be coming down cats and dogs in a minute, and that boy scarcely over the measles!"

Aunt Eleanor laughed.

"Jeremy, this is Emma, who keeps house for me and never stops scolding. She'll scold you, too, if you don't watch out!"

"Only if he deserves it," said Emma. "Don't worry with your case, my dear—I'll bring it. Hurry indoors, both of you! Supper's just ready."

The cottage was a friendly place. The four of them, Jonas, Emma, Jeremy, and Aunt Eleanor, had supper together in the kitchen, which was the biggest room in the house. Jonas lived in the village. He was very old, but he still managed to keep Aunt Eleanor's garden in good order, and he stayed for supper at the cottage two or three evenings a week. Neither he nor Emma was at all respectful to Aunt Eleanor. They ordered her about like a crotchety aunt and uncle; but it was half in fun, and anyone could see that they were very fond of her.

Jeremy disgraced himself by not eating nearly enough to please Emma—or to please himself, either, if it came to that, because they had chicken and strawberries and cream. They all decided that it was because of the measles, and so it was, no doubt; but it may also have been due to the rather queer feeling of excitement that was going on inside him.

When the meal was over Aunt Eleanor took him into the sitting room, and after they had rung up his home to let his parents know that he had arrived safely, she sat down and played the piano. This was something new to Jeremy. There was a radio-phonograph and a television set in his home, but no piano. Miss Wedmore, the music mistress at his school, played tunes for singing and dancing; but he had never before heard anyone play a piano just for fun, playing whatever came into his head.

He enjoyed it, and might have liked it even more if he had been feeling less drowsy. He sat blinking at the oil lamps, which were another novelty. The sitting room was small and warm and full of pictures and books and queer ornaments that looked as though they would be worth examining—but not just then. Aunt Eleanor played pieces that were sometimes gay and sometimes sad, and many of which were by Chopin, although this was something Jeremy did not know; and every now and then there was a patter of raindrops on the window; and Jeremy's head began to nod, and suddenly she exclaimed:

"Jeremy, you're almost asleep! Off you go to bed!"

So off he went. His bedroom was a tiny room with a sloping ceiling and one small window. Emma had unpacked his things, and all he had to do was to pull off his clothes and tumble in. Aunt Eleanor came up a few minutes later to see that he was all right, and he had a twinge of conscience, expecting her to ask if he had remembered to clean his teeth, which he hadn't. But she did not ask any questions. She sat on the edge of the bed, and they talked for two or three minutes about plans and things to do, wondering if the weather would be fine (the rain seemed to be lessening at the moment). Then she went downstairs again, after touching him lightly on the head, as though she had guessed that he did not much like being kissed.

And then Jeremy found, tired as he was, that he could not get to sleep. No doubt this was due partly to the strangeness and newness of everything. Instead, he became more wide awake, and after a while he got out of bed and went to the window, which was partly open. It was still not quite dark. The rain had stopped, and although there were clouds about, a faint glow of sunset lit the sky. He looked over the garden and the paddock. Beyond them the land sloped steeply downward to the little valley along which the river ran. He could not see the river, but on the rising ground on the far side of the valley a gleam of pink caught his eye.

It was the wall of the Old Park, curving away into the distance with nothing to be seen beyond it except the waving tops of trees caught by the last pale glimmer of the sun. This light suddenly vanished, leaving only dusk and shadow behind. For a time Jeremy had almost forgotten about the Park, but now he gazed wistfully toward it, remembering what Aunt Eleanor had said and thinking how marvelous it must once have been. Real wild animals roving in freedom behind that high brick wall —antelope and llamas and kangaroos, and peacocks on the lawns! Were they really all gone? Aunt Eleanor had said that she thought there were still some deer and cattle —and savage, prowling dogs! It seemed very unfair that no one should be allowed in.

The shadows grew deeper and the first stars began to twinkle in the sky. A soft, rainy breeze was blowing in at the window. Jeremy knew he ought to be in bed, and yet he stayed there, scarcely knowing why, gazing through the gathering darkness toward the Park. It was almost as though he were waiting for something to happen; or perhaps he had a faint hope that if he listened he would hear the distant voice of some wild creature prowling beneath the trees.

And suddenly he did hear something, the most unexpected thing in the world. He heard a trumpet call.

It came to him at first so faintly that he could almost believe he had imagined it. But after a minute it was repeated more strongly; and now he was sure that it came from beyond the wall, five clear notes played on a trumpet, so bold and piercing that one seemed almost to be able to see as well as to hear them, like the flash of moonlight on a sword. They sounded like the beginning of a tune—like this:

Who could be playing a trumpet out there in the darkness beneath the trees of the Old Park? Not the caretaker or the men who looked after the animals! Jeremy was suddenly sure of this, although he could not have explained why. Nor did he know why his heart had begun to beat so hard, as though the sound were something magical that had come to him on the breeze.

The trumpet sounded yet again, and now another

thought occurred to him. It was not merely the beginning of a tune; it was really and truly a *call*—a summons—a message expecting an answer. The player paused each time as though awaiting a reply.

Jeremy also waited, almost holding his breath. And presently the reply reached him, but far, far distant, so faint that he could only just hear it, seeming to come from the remotest corner of the Park. It was certainly an answer—five notes, of which the last went up instead of down, like this:

And then there was silence. The first trumpeter, seeming satisfied, did not sound his call again; and after a time Jeremy went back to bed.

He lay with his eyes open, feeling his heart beat and looking toward the window while the thoughts whirled through his mind. He remembered that the real name of the Old Park was Castlecombe, and this was important. The name and the call seemed to go together, and together they conjured up pictures of old and splendid things: of long-fought battles, lances and pennants and the thudding hoofs of chargers; of the great knight, Roland, who had kept the Saracens at bay in the pass of Roncesvalles, not sounding his horn for help till he lay dying; of Robin Hood and his Merry Men amid the Sherwood Forest trees. These were the things Jeremy thought of until at last he curled up and fell happily asleep, feeling strangely certain that he must wait and listen, and that tomorrow or the next day—before many days had passed—he would hear the trumpet call again.

CHAPTER 2

the boy and the arrow

IT RAINED STEADILY FOR THE NEXT TWO days and the morning of the one after, but Jeremy did not mind. He was quite content to spend most of his time indoors, reading or doing jigsaw puzzles, or talking, or listening to the piano, while he rested and got well and strong again, ready for what was coming. He could not have explained to anyone, even to himself, why he was so sure that something was going to happen. It was all to do with the trumpet call, the notes of which were still ringing in his head. He waited, and did not worry because those days passed quietly, with no excitement at all.

He had conversations with Emma in the kitchen and with old Jonas in the garden, when the rain eased. Naturally he asked them about the Old Park, but, like Aunt Eleanor, they seemed not to want to talk about it. Emma had been there in the Old Earl's day, when you paid your shilling to go in, and there were animals in cages and the queerest creatures roaming about—yes, kangaroos and those long-necked llamas, and monkeys, too, quite tame, that came and took your sandwiches if you didn't watch out. It had been lovely then, like a fairy tale almost, but now it was quite changed and she did not know what had become of the animals. Since the Old Earl had gone away, taking the children with him, the place had been shut up as though it were a fortress or a prison, and there were strangers there, and no one knew what went on inside.

"What children?" asked Jeremy.

"His grandchildren, Master Clive and Miss Sally. They used to live there, too, in the Great House, and they'd be in and out the village on their ponies. A nice-looking pair they were. Miss Sally was a pretty little girl, and Master Clive was a tall boy for his age, thin, with a pale sort of face and dark hair—well, a little bit like your auntie, come to think of it. But then they all went to Africa, so I heard, and I suppose they'll be going to school over there, like they would anywhere else."

"But what about the strangers?"

Emma pursed her lips.

"I don't know, Master Jeremy. All I know is that the people who had been working there left soon after the Old Earl went away. They were given their notice—all except Moggs, the caretaker, and his wife, and why those two should have stayed on is more than I can tell you. We never did see much of them in the village, or want to, for that matter. I heard that new people had been brought in to look after the place, but they never show themselves outside, and I don't know anything about them and it's none of my business or yours either, and I haven't time to stand here answering questions. The rain has stopped for the moment. If you want to make yourself useful you can go and pick some strawberries for tea. Mind you see they're ripe on both sides."

This was about all Jeremy managed to get out of Emma. He learned a little more from Jonas, who said that there were certainly still animals in the Park, foreign kinds of cattle and he didn't know what besides. Lately one or two strange birds had flown over the wall, and a monkey had got out and been caught about ten miles away; and when young Jimmy Maddock, from the village, had climbed over the wall one night he had come out again in double-quick time, scared half out of his wits by something that had chased him—not a dog, he wasn't scared of dogs, but some great beast with horns, which wasn't an ordinary bull or cow either; he hadn't waited to see what it was like.

But when Jeremy asked about the new people who had come there, Jonas simply shook his head. They never came to the village. The only time he had set eyes on them was one day when he happened to go past the big, wrought-iron gates and had seen two men in riding breeches, with dark shirts.

"Furriners, that's certain," Jonas said; but, of course, to him all strangers were "foreigners."

Jeremy spent a good deal of his time during the wet days in Aunt Eleanor's studio. She did not mind his being there while she was working and was generally quite ready to talk. He had a table in a corner and did a little drawing on his own account, and now and then she would look over his shoulder when he was in difficulties, and put him right with a flick of her pencil. She was painting a big picture of a river flowing under trees, using sketches and water colors that she had made out-of-doors when the weather was fine. It was fascinating to Jeremy to watch it grow.

On the third day Jeremy brought his whistle with him to the studio, and presently picked it up and softly played "Auld Lang Syne," to show her how he was getting on. Aunt Eleanor said without looking round:

"That was good, Jeremy. What other tunes have you learned?"

He played the six others, tripping up once or twice over "Raggle-Taggle Gypsies," which was the most difficult. Aunt Eleanor glanced at him quickly and smiled. She was concentrating on an awkward bit of the picture, putting on small dabs of color and standing back to see if she was getting it right. Jeremy wished he knew a few more tunes. He put the whistle to his lips again and played the trumpet call.

He did it almost without thinking, having those five notes so much in his mind. Then he played the answer. And suddenly Aunt Eleanor stopped painting and turned to face him.

"Jeremy, where did you hear that?"

"I heard it the night I arrived here," Jeremy said.

"Somebody played it on a trumpet in the Old Park."

"In the Old Park? Are you sure?"

"Yes, quite sure. Have you heard it, too?"

"That's what I'm wondering," said Aunt Eleanor, still looking at him in a puzzled way. "I think it may have been when I was only half listening. But—a trumpet, you said?"

"Yes. There were two people, and they seemed to be calling to one another. One was quite near the wall, I think; but the other was a long way off."

"But who in the world could it have been? Not Moggs, the caretaker, and his wife, that's certain. He's a fat, lazy man who eats and drinks too much, and she's a sly little woman who's always out for what she can get. They wouldn't go running round the Park calling to one another on trumpets, even if they knew how!" Aunt Eleanor laughed at the thought, and then was serious again. "It must have been the men who look after the animals. I don't know how many there are—three or four, I suppose. Perhaps they round up the cattle in the evening. There are avenues, you see, and big open spaces at the center of the Park. The woods are mostly round the edge. Perhaps they do it on horseback, like ranchers in Texas, and use some sort of hunting horn."

Jeremy considered this and shook his head.

"Cattlemen use stock whips. And it was after dark. And anyway it wasn't a bit like that. It was more like a signal. Someone sounded a call and waited for an answer, and while he was waiting everything was quite still. There weren't any sounds of cattle. The one I first heard, the one nearest to me, was in the woods somewhere. That's what it sounded like. He seemed to be dodging about and getting nearer to me. His last call was much clearer. He might have climbed a tree." Jeremy drew a sudden breath. "It could have been a boy," he said.

"Why do you say that?"

"I don't know exactly. I've only just thought of it," said Jeremy. And suddenly he was filled with excitement. "I believe it was a boy."

Aunt Eleanor gazed at him in puzzled silence.

"Have you heard the calls again, since that first night?"

"No," said Jeremy. "But I'm sure I shall."

"Oh, Jeremy, what queer things you say! How can you possibly be sure?"

"I don't know. I know it sounds queer. But I *am* sure."

"And then I suppose you won't be happy till you've found out who the players are?"

"Well, I think I'm going to find out," Jeremy said.

After that they dropped the subject. There is not much sense in trying to explain things you can't explain. Aunt Eleanor was wise enough to understand this; and indeed she was a person who understood a good many things. She turned back to her picture, and after a little while Jeremy strolled out into the garden.

The rain was already stopping. That afternoon the sun came out and old Jonas said, leaning on his hoe:

"Wind's gone north an' turning gentle. I reckon us'll have a fine spell."

Jeremy thought so, too. You could smell fine weather in the air, the way you sometimes can. Aunt Eleanor and he drove four miles to Reddicombe in the pony trap to do some shopping, and then paid one or two calls. They were late getting home, and by the time supper was over the sun was setting. Jeremy said he thought he would go for a stroll.

"All right," said Aunt Eleanor. "It's turned lovely and warm." She did not ask where he was going.

Jeremy knew exactly where he was going. He had found the place the day before, when he had gone out for a quick walk between showers. It was a little knoll, a hump of land with a single tree upon it, just at the foot of the hillside where it reached the river's edge. Jeremy climbed to the highest point, a few yards from the tree, and sat down on the rough grass. He had brought his whistle with him.

Directly in front of him was the river, flowing fast because its waters had been swollen by the rain. Beyond the river was the footpath, and beyond the footpath was the high brick wall, with the dense trees of the Old Park rising up behind it. There was no bridge.

Jeremy sat waiting while the shadows grew longer. He had an idea that the trumpets were never blown by daylight, and that he must not expect to hear them until the sun was gone. He did not know whether he was going to hear them again that evening; but he knew that he must listen for them whenever he had the chance.

So he waited patiently with his whistle in his hand.

The sun sank lower and vanished at last beyond the ridge of hills over to the west. For a time there was a glow in the sky, a pale orange light hiding the darkness, and then this, too, suddenly vanished.

Jeremy sat without moving in the cool, silvery afterglow, with the sky turning to purple and the first stars showing. The evening was very still and so quiet that the ripple of the river sounded very loud and he could hear a cow lowing in a field that must, he knew, be at least half a mile away. When suddenly he heard the first trumpet it made him start a little, but he was not really surprised.

The trumpet played the same five notes as before—the call, the summons. And Jeremy sat upright and did what he had planned to do. He played the answer on his whistle.

The note of a tin whistle is not a very loud one, but he made it as shrill and piercing as he could, praying that it would carry far enough. Then, with his heart wildly beating, he sat and waited, wondering if the second trumpet would answer as well.

It did so after a few moments, sounding far distant. Jeremy had a queer feeling of distress. He thought, "Perhaps they'll only listen to each other, and not take any notice of me!" Nevertheless, he played the answering call again.

He played it four times altogether before anything else happened. Then, suddenly, the first trumpet sounded much more loudly, and he realized that the player must

have been moving in his direction. At once he played the answer again, and the trumpet sounded immediately after it, playing two quick notes, as though to say, "I've heard you. I'm coming."

Jeremy stood up so that he could be seen by anyone who might climb one of the trees beyond the wall. It was still not quite dark. The world was sinking rapidly into the state of twilight in which you can see only light and shadow, without ever being sure what the shadows are. Jeremy could still see the wall quite clearly, and beyond it the dark blur of treetops; he could not expect to see anyone who might be amid the branches.

After a while he heard a faint sound which might have been that of a person climbing a tree. He could not tell. It might have been a monkey or a bird, or just nothing. He stayed quite still while the darkness deepened. In a few minutes the wall would be invisible, which meant that he would be almost invisible, too, although, standing out in the open in his white shirt, he would stay visible a good deal longer than the wall.

And then he saw a light that gleamed and vanished. It presently showed again, jerking like a will-o'-the-wisp high in the trees. At last it came to rest, glowing steadily, just a tiny pool of light shining through leaves and branches, but revealing nothing else. Jeremy could not stay quiet any longer. He called:

"Who's there?"

The reply came at once, from just the other side of the wall, forty or fifty yards away.

"A friend. Wait for the arrow. Don't call again."

It was a boy's voice.

Jeremy waited for what seemed a very long time. The minutes dragged past. Suddenly there was a little thud close beside him, and he looked down and saw a long, slender shape quivering in the ground almost at his feet.

He bent down quickly and picked it up. The light had vanished. After a moment the trumpet sounded—two quick notes. Then there was silence.

Jeremy found that there was a scrap of paper tied to the shaft of the arrow with threads that might have been torn from a handkerchief. It was far too dark to read what was written on it, so he turned and went back to the cottage.

Aunt Eleanor was at her desk in the sitting room, writing letters. She glanced at him as he came in.

"Was it nice out?"

"Yes," said Jeremy, "it was—it was very nice."

She gave him a quick look and went on writing.

Jeremy had had a chance to examine the arrow on his way back. It was a real one, made for business, with a proper bone nock at the feathered end and a sharp steel point. He had left it in the hall stand, to take upstairs when he went to bed.

He sat down and unfolded the scrap of paper, which was dirty and very creased. The message, scrawled in pencil, read as follows:

"If you're a friend come to the place where the river

runs under the wall. Ten o'clock tomorrow morning. This is secret. We need friends."

After reading it twice Jeremy folded it and put it in his pocket. Then he found that Aunt Eleanor was again looking at him.

"Jeremy, what's happened?"

"I—I had a message," said Jeremy awkwardly. "But it's secret."

"Oh," said Aunt Eleanor.

Jeremy felt that he had to tell her, because it would be unfair not to. In any case, he felt sure that if the boy had known her he would not have minded.

"I was right about it being a boy who sounded the trumpet call," he said. "He spoke to me. And he sent a message tied to an arrow."

"An arrow! But, Jeremy, who is he?"

"I don't know. I was wondering—do you think it could be the Old Earl's grandson? He didn't sound like a village boy."

"But they all went abroad. If they'd come back, the village people would be sure to know."

"He said it was secret," said Jeremy. "And he asked me to meet him at a place tomorrow morning, because they need friends."

"Does that mean that you're going into the Park?"

"Well, he didn't say so, but—"

"That's what you want to do, isn't it?"

Jeremy nodded. After a little pause he said slowly:

"Of course I won't if you say I mustn't, but—" He was

watching Aunt Eleanor's face, and he thought he saw the beginning of a smile at the corners of her mouth. He went on boldly: "You know *you'd* go, if you were me!"

At this she had to laugh.

"A secret boy in the Park who sends messages tied to arrows!" she said softly. "I'd go like a shot! Oh, dear, Jeremy, I don't know what your parents would say. You mustn't stay too long."

"Perhaps I'll send *you* a message tied to an arrow," Jeremy said.

CHAPTER 3

under the wall!

AT A LITTLE BEFORE TEN THE NEXT MORNING Jeremy sat down on a tuft of grass a few yards from the high brick wall of the Park, with the river at his feet. The river ran under a low archway in the wall, a single span about ten yards across, which was built out much wider than the wall itself, like a small bridge. The river-bank, on the side where Jeremy was seated, with the wall at his right, was steep and thickly overgrown with bushes. He had had to do a good deal of scrambling and wading through the water's edge to get to this place; but since he was wearing sneakers and his oldest gray school shirt and shorts, this did not matter.

He was also wearing a belt with his clasp knife attached to it, and over his shoulder he had a shopping bag with a long strap, belonging to Aunt Eleanor, which contained his whistle and a parcel of food. Aunt Eleanor had said he had better take this in case he did not come back to the cottage for lunch. She herself was going to spend the whole day out-of-doors, walking and sketching. She and

Jeremy had started off together, leaving Emma to suppose that they would be together all day, and thus keeping Jeremy's expedition a secret. And when they had reached the river they had separated, Aunt Eleanor going to the left, to wander wherever the fancy took her, and Jeremy going to the right and making his way upstream.

"Remember," Aunt Eleanor had said, "if you aren't back by suppertime I shall have to do something about it. I'm responsible for you, don't forget."

"I know," said Jeremy. "I expect I'll be back. But if anything *should* happen I'll try and send a message." He pointed to the knoll where he had sat the night before. "You'll find an arrow sticking into the trunk of that tree, or anyway very close to it."

"Well . . ." said Aunt Eleanor. "All right. But take care of yourself."

She had given him a little smile which touched Jeremy's heart, because she understood how important it all was. For a moment he had almost wished she was coming, too.

And now he sat waiting beneath a warm sun and a serene blue sky which gave promise of a perfect day. The river swirled and bubbled past, looking green and deep at this point, where its bed was a good deal narrower than it was lower down. On the other side was the foot-path, and there was a door in the wall, just beyond the archway, to which this path led. It was a solid-looking door, set in a small archway of its own with iron spikes at the top, and Jeremy kept glancing at it, wondering whether it would suddenly open and a boy come out. If this was the way he was to be let into the Park he would have to swim across the river, because the nearest bridge, as he knew, was more than a mile lower down. But the thought did not worry him. He had learned to swim two years ago, and by practicing hard last year had got to be quite good at it.

He was doing his best to keep calm, although he was quivering with excitement inside. Fishes kept jumping in the river, birds darted above it, swarms of midges hung over it, and those queer daddy longlegs flies, that are sometimes called "boatmen," went skidding about on the surface. With the hot sun upon him, the warmth, the waiting, the flow and ripple of the water, Jeremy began to feel as though he were in a dream. And suddenly a voice called:

"Is anybody there?"

It was the boy's voice, but it sounded strangely different, filled with echoes and mingled with the sounds of the river. It seemed to come from under the archway.

Jeremy jumped up at once and scrambled along until he was peering under the archway with one foot in the river. It was like looking through a low tunnel about eight feet long; and as Jeremy now saw there was a crisscross of iron bars across the middle, reaching down into the water, with dead leaves and branches swept up against it on the other side. It took Jeremy a few moments to make out the head of a boy amid these branches. He was hanging on to the iron grille in midstream, with most of his body under water.

"I'm here!" said Jeremy, his voice echoing.

"Do you want to come in?"

"Yes."

"It's dangerous. I've got to warn you of that."

"I don't care," said Jeremy, without hesitating. He had known that it would be dangerous. "I want to come."

"All right. You'll have to come this way because the door's padlocked. Can you swim?"

"Yes."

"But under water? There's this barrier, you see—it's to stop the water birds and animals getting out. It goes down to within about two feet of the bottom. The water's only about six feet deep, but the current's pretty strong."

"Oh," said Jeremy.

"It won't be too bad. Once you've managed to wriggle a bit of the way I'll grab hold of you and pull. It'll only take a second."

"All right," said Jeremy. "But I've got a bag with sandwiches. They'll be spoiled."

"Throw it over the wall. And hurry! The rain's made the river jolly cold!"

Jeremy took off his belt and put it in the bag. He stood back from the wall, where it climbed up the steep, high bank on his side of the river, and tossed the bag over. Then he went back to the archway and for a moment hesitated, looking at the flowing water and the grille.

"Keep to the side," said the boy. "The current won't be quite so strong."

Taking a deep breath, Jeremy dived in. The fact was

that although he had started diving last year, he had never swum more than two strokes under water. But this was one of those things you have to do at once, without hesitating. He dived in and swam downward and forward with all his strength, while the river fought to drive him back.

The river was much stronger than he was; but the impetus of his dive and two lusty kicks were enough to bring him to the barrier. And then came the really hard part. He had to force himself underneath, turning a little on his side to do so and pulling on the round iron bar that ran along the bottom of the grille, with his chest bursting, and muddy green darkness in his eyes and the rush of the river in his ears. Probably the whole thing did not take more than half a minute, but it was the longest half-minute Jeremy had ever known. Suddenly he felt a hand grip him beneath the armpit. He was dragged forward, and an instant later he bobbed to the surface amid the dead branches.

He hung on to the bars, gasping and spluttering, and the boy looked at him anxiously.

"Are you all right? Are you sure you're all right?"

"Yes," said Jeremy breathlessly. "I'm all right. But, gosh—!"

"It was pretty awful, wasn't it, just for a second? I knew it would be. I didn't dare tell you. That current's pretty strong. I think you're jolly good!"

The boy then began to try to shift some of the branches.

"This lumber's a nuisance," he said. "We've got to get

over to the other side. Never mind—hang on to me and we'll manage."

He seemed to be very strong and clever. With Jeremy hanging on to his shoulders, he got them somehow through the tangle of branches and safely onto the opposite bank.

"Now you can have a rest, but you mustn't stop here. Nip across the bridle path and sit under that tree, and if you get a warning, bolt into the wood. We have to keep under cover, you see, as much as we can. I'll get your bag."

Jeremy did as he was told, and sat down beneath an oak tree on the other side of the bridle path, which ran alongside the river and then curved round to follow the wall. He sat facing the river, with the ground rising gradually behind him into a rough tangle of tree and bush and rock, with bluebells growing here and there. On the other side of the river the land rose more steeply but looked much tidier, being planted with young larch and pine. The bridle path was broad and grassy, and bore recent hoof marks. The river wound away into the distance on Jeremy's left, and at his right hand vanished abruptly under the archway. Beside the archway was the door in the wall, which was secured not only by a rusty bolt but by a bright new padlock.

Jeremy absorbed these details gradually. At the moment he was more interested in watching the boy, who was walking a few yards upstream to allow for the current. He looked about fifteen, a tall, wiry, dark-haired boy with a thin face tanned almost coffee color by the sun. He wore trunks, and his clothes lay under the tree where Jeremy was sitting. He dived into the river and swam across under water, bobbing up on the other side and springing onto the bank in a single movement, like an otter. After searching for a few moments he found Jeremy's bag and swam across with it, holding it clear of the water.

Jeremy had discovered that one of his legs was bleeding. He must have scraped it scrambling under the barrier. It was smarting a bit. The boy knelt down beside him and said:

"That's quite a bad gash. It ought to be wrapped up." Then he surprised Jeremy by suddenly shouting: "Hey, Sal, come on down!"

Jeremy looked round quickly and saw a pair of brown legs descending a tree not far away. They were followed by blue shorts, a yellow jersey, and finally the head of a girl as sunburned as the boy, with hair of a lighter brown. She was about Jeremy's size and age. But the most interesting thing about her, at first sight, was that she carried a bow in her hand and had a quiver filled with arrows hanging from her shoulder.

"No sign of anyone?" asked the boy.

"No, it seems to be all right. But I don't like this place, Clive—it's too open. And you can see they use the bridle path. We ought to get away from here."

"I know. But first this boy's leg wants tying up. Did you see him dive under the barrier? He's jolly good. You'd better tear a strip off my shirt—it's fairly clean."

"Well, put your trousers on, anyway," the girl said. "And stop calling him 'this boy'! How rude you are, Clive!" She was tearing a strip off the tail of the shirt as she spoke, and she turned to Jeremy with a warm and friendly smile which made him like her at once. "What's your name?"

"Jeremy Shepherd."

"Jeremy!" said the boy. "I'm a Jeremy, too. There have been lots in our family—of course, it's Jeremiah really. I've got a whole row of Christian names—Lancelot

Xavier Jeremy Sebastian Clive Nicholas. Clive's the one I use."

"And my names are Henrietta Charlotte Katherine Sarah Guinevere, but I'm called Sally," the girl said. "We rather run to names in our family."

"You're the Old Earl's grandchildren, aren't you?" said Jeremy.

They glanced at one another.

"We thought you probably wouldn't know that," Clive said, "because you're fairly new in these parts, aren't you? Yes, we're Clive and Sally Palfrey. But it mustn't be talked about, because we aren't supposed to be here."

"I won't say anything," said Jeremy.

He had got his breath by now, and was feeling warm in spite of his wet clothes. He was glowing with excitement and triumph and happiness, because he had got here, and everything had happened as he had known that it would.

He watched the two Palfreys while Sally quickly cleaned and bandaged his leg and Clive pulled on a pair of very worn flannel slacks. Clive had a belt to which was attached a long sheath knife—a real hunting knife. He also had something that rather surprised Jeremy—a big, metal-framed catapult. Seeing Jeremy's eyes upon this he grinned and pulled a handful of half-inch ball bearings out of his pocket.

"This is my ammunition. Our weapons are a bit old-fashioned. We've just had to use what we could lay our hands on. But they're more effective than you might think."

A thousand questions trembled on Jeremy's lips, but before he could say anything more he was caused to look up by a strange sound coming from immediately above their heads. A small brown monkey was perched on the branch of the tree, peering down at them and chattering furiously.

"Tiresome little creature!" said Sally, glancing up. "It must have been following us. Those things'll give us away if we aren't careful, Clive. I believe that's why they've let them out."

"Are there many?" asked Jeremy, gazing at it in wonderment.

"Quite a lot. We used to let out a few in the old days, but they were half tame, and they'd come to the house for food, so we could round them up. But now the keepers seem to have just opened the enclosure and let them all out. It's a shame! They'll lose most of them. The poor little things will stray, or die when the winter comes."

Clive had put on a pair of sandals and was now pulling the remains of his shirt over his head. He shook his fist at the monkey, but he did not shoot at it with his catapult. He fastened his belt, glancing about him as he did so, and seeming to listen. Both the Palfreys were very quick in their movements, very intent and alert, seeming to be always on the watch, so that Jeremy did not like to bother them with questions.

Sally jumped to her feet.

"Now we're ready," she said. "Are we going to the sycamore?"

"Yes," said Clive. "I want to see if anything's happening at the house. Mickey said he'd be back soon after midday. I hope he's got the fireworks."

"We must have been a good hour getting here from the cave," said Sally.

Jeremy's eyes opened wide. Things were getting more and more puzzling and mysterious.

"Do you live in a cave?" he asked.

"Yes. Almost on the other side of the Park. You'll see."

"And it took you an hour to get here!" Jeremy exclaimed. "The Park must be enormous!"

"It is," said Sally. "It's bigger than it looks from outside—much bigger. And everything's different when you're inside. You'll find that out." She gave him a quick smile. "Are you just bursting to be told about everything? There's so much of it, and we can't talk here. You'll have to wait till we get to the sycamore."

"Come on," said Clive.

CHAPTER 4

the black dog

AFTER THEY HAD GONE A SHORT DISTANCE the ground began to rise more steeply. The Park was a valley, girdled with hills, with the river flowing through it; a huge bowl, roughly oval in shape, with a rim composed of a series of high ridges broken by occasional folds. These natural ramparts were thickly wooded, with the wall running round their outskirts. There was no point outside from which one could see the open grassland at the center of the Park, or the great house which was its heart, even if one climbed to the top of the wall.

They were passing along the crests of the southern ridges, through a jungle of trees and undergrowth, following little paths, deer and badger tracks.

"We have to keep where it's thickest," Sally said. "It gets much more open toward the center, and there are the 'vistas'—five huge, straight, grassy avenues, all about a mile long, running to the house like the spokes of a wheel. We daren't cross them by daylight because of the risk of being seen."

"Who is it you're afraid of?" asked Jeremy.

"The keepers. They're our enemies."

"But how many of them are there?"

"We haven't been able to find out for certain. Nine or ten, at least. And there are some gardeners, but they don't count. And there's Moggs, the caretaker, and his wife. They're the only ones who were here before we went away. Moggs was steward and his wife was housekeeper. But they're traitors. We know we can't trust them."

Nine or ten keepers! Aunt Eleanor had said she thought there might be three or four. Everything became larger once you were inside the walls!

But it seemed that in these days the keepers were more concerned with keeping people out of the Park than with looking after the animals, of which there were still a large number, although most of the rarer kinds were gone. The caged animals had all been sold, and there were no longer any llamas or kangaroos; but there were still foreign breeds of cattle and sheep among the herds that grazed around the house. There were red deer running through the woods, and several kinds of antelope, and Canadian moose, which in the old days had been kept in their own enclosure because of the damage they did to trees. They were now running wild with the rest, and it was probably one of these awkward creatures, with their huge antlers, which had frightened the village boy who had climbed over the wall.

But there were worse things. The boar pen had been opened; and above all there were the dogs. . . . The Old

Park had become a sort of jungle, dangerous to man and beast alike. All this had happened since the Old Earl and his grandchildren went away. Perhaps it was due partly to the carelessness and heartlessness of the people in charge, but there were other reasons as well.

Jeremy had to make what he could of the scraps of information Sally let fall, speaking in a cool, quiet, matter-of-fact voice, as though there were nothing unusual in all this. She had her bow strung and an arrow ready. She never relaxed her watchfulness for an instant. But she did not seem at all afraid.

A sudden screech caused them to look up, and they saw a brightly plumaged bird flying away through the tops of the trees. Clive, who was about fifteen yards in front, waited for them to come up with him and said:

"A macaw. They must have opened the aviary."

"The birds will simply fly away," said Sally.

"Yes, in the end, but they may hang about the Park for some days before they do. And while they do they're a danger to us, just like the monkeys. The keepers are doing everything they can to find us. Things are hotting up, Sal. Move quietly, and keep your voice very low if you have to talk."

He went on again and they followed in silence. It was rough, tangled going along the crest of the ridge, but at least it was tolerably safe from the keepers, who rode horses and were more or less confined to the bridle paths. Jeremy had moments of feeling he was walking through a strange country, not England at all. He kept seeing things he had never seen before, trees of kinds unknown to him, flowering shrubs with bright blossoms and strange scents, small animals that darted away at their approach, skunks, opossums, and raccoons, and once a splendid antlered stag who stood gazing at them for a moment, quite close, and then went bounding away—a ten-pointer, Sally said.

Suddenly there was an emergency. As they broke onto a path leading to a small clearing they saw that Clive was standing motionless with his back to them, his hand raised in warning above his head. He was looking at something in the clearing. After a moment he walked forward, moving slowly, with his catapult in his hand. They followed cautiously, Sally with an arrow in her bow and Jeremy clutching his open clasp knife, which was the only weapon he had.

They heard a sound of snuffling and growling, a rather horrible sound. When they had gone a little farther they saw in the center of the clearing a huge black dog standing over the carcass of a young deer. The dog was a pure-bred English mastiff, a breed that is almost extinct. It was tearing at the carcass with blood running from its jowls; but suddenly it looked up at Clive, who was walking quietly round the edge of the clearing with his eyes fixed upon it. It gave a low, terrifying growl, and the hair rose on its back. Clive said in a calm, steady voice:

"Hallo, Prince! So you've had to kill your dinner! Don't they feed you nowadays?" He went on without any change of tone: "Follow me round, you two. Keep your eyes on him but don't look frightened. *Don't be afraid!"*

Sally at once began to walk round, speaking to the dog in the same quiet voice:

"Naughty Prince to kill a fawn! Couldn't you have got a goat instead?" She went on, to Jeremy, who was following behind her: "There used to be three of them. They were house dogs. They were darlings, the gentlest creatures in the world! The keepers must have deliberately starved him to make him savage. I think this is the beastliest thing they've done! . . . Clive, we shall have to kill him if he comes for us."

"I know," said Clive. "But it'll be all right if we keep our heads. Go on with your dinner, Prince, you naughty old boy!"

The dog did not move toward them. He stood with his feet straddling his prey, watching them as they went past, growling and then whining, as though in the end he was more puzzled than angry. Finally they pushed their way through a thicket on the far side of the clearing.

"He won't come after us," said Clive. "Too keen on his grub. He—" He was interrupted by the sudden barking of the dog, several deep, baying barks, loud enough to be heard half a mile away. "Blast! We mastered him, and so he has to show off! We'd better—"

Sally clutched his arm. They stood listening to the sound of horses' hoofs, near and coming rapidly nearer.

Things happened very quickly. Almost before he knew it, Jeremy was dragged down by Sally into the cover of the thicket, while at the same instant Clive leaped up into the branches of a tree overlooking the clearing, moving with an extraordinary speed and nimbleness.

The hoofbeats were now very near, and suddenly a black horse thundered into the clearing, ridden by a man with a dark, surly face. He wore riding breeches and a dark-blue shirt, and he had a rifle or shotgun in a long holster and carried a coiled whip in his hand.

He reined his horse, looking down at the dog, which was now growling furiously. Without paying any attention to it, he sat glancing keenly about him. Suddenly he uttered a sharp cry and rocked in his saddle, nearly falling off. He had been hit on the head by something. To be exact, he had been hit by a half-inch ball bearing propelled at short range by a powerful catapult.

Clive fired two more shots, both at the horse, causing it to rear up, whinnying madly. It bolted, crashing away along the path by which it had come, while its rider sagged over its neck, seeming half stunned by the blow on the head.

"That'll teach 'em to starve the dogs!" Clive said.

He jumped down from the tree, his eyes bright and his mouth smiling—a fierce, angry grin.

"Come on! We've got to get to the sycamore!"

"That's the first time we've actually attacked a keeper," said Sally as they ran. "That man'll be badly hurt if he falls off."

"Can't help it. He'd have spotted us in another minute. Don't talk any more."

The sycamore was still about half a mile away, but they

reached it without any further trouble, covering the ground at a steady trot.

It was a great and noble tree, standing a little below the crest of the southern ridge, with lesser trees all round it. The massive trunk soared upward, its lowest branch twenty feet above the ground. But while Jeremy was wondering how in the world they were to climb it, Clive had plunged into the bushes, from which he emerged with a coil of rope with a heavy metal ring spliced into one end. He tossed this over one of the great outflung branches of the tree, lowered it on the other side, passed the other end of the rope through the ring, and pulled it tight.

"Up you go!" he said to Sally; and to Jeremy: "You next!"

Sally went up like a monkey. Jeremy followed more slowly—like any boy who has learned to climb a rope in the school gymnasium. Clive came up hand over hand, without troubling to use his legs.

When he had reached the branch Clive loosened the rope, coiled it neatly, and laid it in the bole of the tree. Sally, meanwhile, was climbing higher, and Jeremy followed, finding it difficult at first because the branches were widely spaced. The tree was gigantic. High above the ground, and nearly on a level with the tops of the surrounding trees, there was a spread of three branches. Saplings had been laid across these and lashed with cord, making a sort of bird's nest where three people might sit in comfort and safety, almost invisible from the ground.

Some bits of sacking had been arranged to make this

nest more comfortable still. Sally sat down, and Jeremy was about to do the same when Clive said:

"The observation post's a bit higher, if you want to have a look at the house."

"Please!" said Jeremy. Breathless though he was, he could not rest until he had seen everything.

He unslung his shopping bag, and then, remembering its contents, offered the picnic parcel to Sally.

"Sandwiches!" she cried. "Oh—heaven!"

"Don't wolf the lot!" said Clive.

The thought occurred to Jeremy that it must be only about two hours since Aunt Eleanor had given him those sandwiches. He could scarcely believe it. He felt already as though he had been in the Park for days.

He followed Clive up a high-soaring branch, still sheltered by the big, protecting leaves of the sycamore. Clive was getting a pair of binoculars out of a leather case which had evidently been left up there, standing with his foot in the fork of a smaller branch and his arm round the main stem.

"This is about as high as we can go without the risk of being spotted," he said. "They may have glasses of their own."

"Why are they so frantically keen to catch you?" asked Jeremy. "Why are they enemies?"

"Oh, well, that's part of the story. We'll tell you in a little while. . . ." Clive now had the glasses to his eyes. After a few moments he uttered an exclamation. "Hullo! There's two of them helping a third toward the house!

And there's another leading a horse. Do you hear that, Sal? That chap I hit must have taken a toss, after all! He's looking pretty shaky. Well, that ought to stir them up!"

He continued to watch through the glasses for another two or three minutes, and then said:

"They've gone in now. There doesn't seem to be anything else happening. Come up if you want to look."

He slipped down to let Jeremy take his place, handing him the glasses. Jeremy found that there was a gap in the leaves through which he could see the tops of the surrounding trees. The ground sloped gently downward, and about a quarter of a mile from where he was perched the woods ended, giving place to a wide, rolling expanse of open parkland. At the center of this, surrounded by hedges and terraces, lawns and gardens, stood the great house of Castlecombe.

The grassy spaces, with here and there a big, isolated tree, were dotted with the forms of grazing animals, cattle and sheep of many different kinds. For a moment Jeremy's attention was held by these. Clive's voice said from below him:

"You can't see the menagerie buildings, they're all on the far side. All you can see from here is the house itself. There's enough of it, you must admit."

Jeremy looked at the house.

His first feeling was that he was not looking at one house at all, but at a group of houses, of different styles and shapes and sizes, clustered in a disorderly way around several inner courtyards or quadrangles. Somewhere about the center was a massive stone tower like that of a medieval fortress, which indeed is what it was. And the front part of the house was a mansion with a pillared portico and two unequal wings, sweeping forward like arms to embrace an outer courtyard from which steps descended to a formal, terraced garden flanked by carriage drives.

It was like a village, almost; a small township, without any semblance of a plan. It was beautiful in many of its parts, but quite disorderly as a whole; and beautiful again because of the weathered mellowness of stone and brick and tiles and timber, which made one think of a huge, sprawling plant that had sprung in its own untidy fashion out of the earth. Nor was this so very far from the truth. Starting with that square fortress tower it had grown piece by piece, added to by successive generations of builders over a period of nearly six hundred years.

"It's like our family," Clive murmured. "Sort of casual. They've been great ones for building and adding and improving, but they couldn't bear to pull anything down."

"It's—it's enormous!" Jeremy said.

"Yes. The monstrous old dump!" There was love as well as laughter in Clive's voice. "There are two hundred and eleven rooms, including the servants' quarters but not counting the attics and cellars. There's a Great Hall and a Banqueting Hall, and nine drawing rooms, and a ballroom and a gun room and a trophy room and a fencing hall and a library, which is four rooms knocked into one, and a picture gallery and a museum, and—oh, well, everything else you can think of, including things like a bakery and joinery, and a smithy and a weaving room. And a chapel, of course. You can see the belfry on this side. It's got a huge bell. And the place is full of old furniture and family portraits, and jolly dingy they are, most of them. And *we* think it's full of ghosts, although other people don't seem to notice them. They're just the family, you see—great-great-great-grandfathers and grandmothers and uncles and aunts and cousins. It has all belonged to our family since the fourteenth century; but unless Sal and I can find the things we're looking for by the end of this month, which is in nine days' time, it won't belong to us any more."

"What are you looking for?"

"For two things," said Clive. "We're on a quest. We're looking for a Casket and a Sword."

Jeremy stayed quite still for some time while he took all this in. He glanced down at Clive and saw that his face was serious. At last he said:

"And the keepers are here to prevent you?"

"Yes. We're pretty outnumbered, I admit, but we have some advantages. And we have one very good friend. His name's Mickey Few. You'll be meeting him soon. We badly needed one or two more to help with the plan we've been preparing. We had a feeling someone would turn up, but it was rather wonderful when you answered the trumpet call."

"I heard it the first night I got here," said Jeremy slowly. "The night the rain began. I knew I had to listen and I'd hear it again. I somehow knew I'd be coming here. But I've no idea how I knew."

"Castlecombe is like that," said Clive. "It's so old. It makes you know all kinds of things. That's to say, it does if you're the right kind of person. But if you aren't, you're lost. That's what I meant when I said we had advantages over the keepers. We belong here, and they don't. They don't know or understand anything. They make mistakes all the time."

At this moment there was an interruption from below. Sally was not so far away that she could not hear what they were saying. She had been ferreting inquisitively in Jeremy's bag and had found his whistle. As though joining in the conversation she played the trumpet call and the answer.

"Steady on, Sal," said Clive. "You don't know who may be near."

"It's all right. There're two monkeys here—two capuchins. I've got them on our side by giving them Jeremy's banana—sorry, Jeremy! They'll soon let us know if anyone comes this way."

Clive climbed up into Jeremy's place, taking the glasses from him, and Jeremy came down to the lower branch. Peering through the leaves, he could see Sally's upturned face above the yellow jersey.

"Do you know something, Clive?" she said. "Mickey and I have done the song."

Clive had the glasses directed toward the house.

"Oh, good," he said, not paying much attention.

"What song?" asked Jeremy.

"The trumpet-call song. We use the trumpets for keeping in touch after dark, among other things. But we first learned to play them for a pageant about three years ago. We had to play that call and the answer. I always did feel that it ought to be made into a song. And yesterday, when Mickey Few and I were alone together in the cave, it sort of came to us."

"Sing it!" said Jeremy.

"Not too loud!" said Clive.

"Fuss pot!" said Sally; and she sang:

> "When the shades are falling
> Deep beneath the trees,
> Hear the trumpet calling
> Like silver on the breeze!
> You must call in answer—never, never fail;
> We must seek and find before the shadows pale!
> Brothers of the woods
> Harken to my cry;
> We must fight and conquer,
> We must do or die!"

Sally's sweet, clear voice came winging up to them like the song of a bird amid the treetops. And a surprising thing happened to Jeremy. For an instant he felt a lump in his throat. He did not know why he found that little song so lovely and exciting, or why he was sure that he would remember it all his life.

There was a silence, and then Clive said:

"The tune isn't so bad, but the words are a bit silly, if you ask me."

"That's mean!" said Sally hotly. "The words are always more difficult when the tune comes first. What's wrong with them, anyway?"

"Well, they're exaggerated, for one thing. All that about fighting and conquering, and doing or dying. Anyone would think this was the battle of Agincourt!"

"Well, it's a battle about old things, and you know it is. And anyway, those are the sort of words you want for a trumpet tune."

"Yes," said Clive, "but—"

Then he broke off. He had had the glasses to his eyes the whole time.

"Four keepers on horses!" he exclaimed. "And they've got— Good Lord! Sal, they've got bloodhounds!"

"Bloodhounds! Clive, they can't be! We've never had bloodhounds at Castlecombe."

"Well, they've got some now. They must have brought them in from outside. Perhaps they've just been waiting for a chance to use them. They're moving over to our right—I can guess where they're making for!"

"But what good will they do? If they can't give them our scent they won't get anywhere."

"I know. Perhaps they haven't thought of that. They may be just furious because I wanged one of them on the head. Things really are hotting up! That song of yours isn't so far out, Sal! It's a real battle now!"

CHAPTER 5

the bloodhounds

"WE'LL STAY HERE TILL THE EXCITEMENT dies down," said Clive. "We mustn't risk being trailed to the cave. I'm glad about these sandwiches."

They were all together now in their bird's nest, warm and comfortable and well hidden. Two small gray monkeys with black fringed faces were seated side by side on a nearby branch, looking like two little old men begging for alms. Jeremy did not know which was more strange, the presence of the monkeys or the fact that they should be sitting there, calmly eating his sandwiches, while the hunt for them went on in the distance, with the baying, snuffling hounds and the dark-shirted riders armed with whips and guns.

But the Palfreys were quite unperturbed. As Clive said, if it was the injury to the keeper that had brought them out, they would be bound to start by going to the clearing where it had happened, and this was a good half-mile from the sycamore.

"And then what will they do?" said Clive. "Bloodhounds are no use unless they're given a definite scent to follow—something a person has worn. They'll just snuffle round in circles. Those keepers are stupid. They don't understand things. The more they panic the better it will be for us."

"But why, exactly?" asked Jeremy. "You know, you've scarcely told me anything yet."

"Poor Jeremy!" said Sally. "He's simply exploding with questions, and it's all so complicated! Come to that, Jeremy, we don't know anything about you either, except your name."

"And we know you're all right," said Clive.

Jeremy blushed and told them about the measles and Aunt Eleanor, and also the little he had heard about Castlecombe. Clive said:

"You've got it more or less right. Our father was killed in the war, you see, and afterward our mother married again and went to live in America, and since then we've lived here with Grandfather. But it wasn't Grandfather who started the menagerie. That's much older. The Palfreys are a queer sort of family, very like one another in some ways and very different in others. Some have been generals and ambassadors and important things like that, and others have been adventurers and pirates; and some have just wandered about the world, doing nothing special, and others have stayed at home, building and improving Castlecombe. The menagerie was started by Grandfather's grandfather, who was a hunter and animal collector and became quite famous as a zoologist. His son carried it on, although I don't think he was really very interested. Then it was Grandfather's turn, and he cares more about animals than about anything else in the world."

"But not as a hunter," said Sally. "He hates killing them or even caging them, if it can be avoided. That's why he built the wall, so that as many as possible could run free. Grandfather's very sweet, and some people think he's a bit mad, but we know he's just a woolgatherer. Anyway, it was the wall that ruined him. It goes right round, you see. It took two years to build. It's nine feet high and nearly fifteen miles long. The expense must have been enormous."

Although he was growing used to the size of Castlecombe, Jeremy could not help gasping at this.

"Yes," said Clive with a faint grin. "Fifteen miles of wall!"

He sat listening for a moment to the distant baying of the bloodhounds floating up to them on the warm, still air. "They're not getting any nearer," he said. He broke one of the biscuits Aunt Eleanor had so thoughtfully provided, and tossed the pieces to the monkeys, who caught them very skillfully. Then he went on:

"Well, what happened was that one day nearly three years ago Grandfather woke up and found that he was broke. Of course, he'd really been going broke for a long time, but he hadn't noticed. I suppose when you've got the habit of being very rich you don't think about money like ordinary people, you just spend it. Grandfather had managed to spend everything there was. In fact, it was even worse than that, because he'd borrowed an awful lot from a man in London called Mungo McDougal. He's the villain of the story. But we didn't know about him then. All we knew was that one morning Grandfather came down to breakfast and said that we were going to close down Castlecombe and go to Africa, to find a diamond mine and repair the family fortunes."

"Which shows you how much of a woolgatherer he is," said Sally, with a soft laugh. "It's no use thinking that you've only got to go to Africa and you'll just sort of trip over a diamond mine. We know that now, but at the time we didn't understand what it was all about. We just thought it was wonderful to be going to Africa."

"And so it was," said Clive. "It's been marvelous. We spent nearly the whole time on safari, trekking all over the place—Kenya, Tanganyika, the Belgian Congo, Nigeria, Uganda. But never a sniff of a diamond mine! Half the time we weren't even trying. We were in the game reserves, and Grandfather was filming animals and trapping rare specimens to send back to England, and I shot a leopard and—" Clive broke off with a little sigh. "Oh, well! I think Grandfather had an idea that something or other would turn up to save us, but of course it didn't, and he began to get very depressed and miserable. In the end he told us all about the money he owed, and that if it wasn't paid back by the end of June the whole of Castlecombe, the house and Park and everything, would go to this man

McDougal. It was the beginning of May when he told us. That was less than two months ago."

"Gosh!" said Jeremy. "How awful!"

"Yes," said Clive. "And there we were, not far from Nairobi, pretending to look for a diamond mine that we hadn't a hope of finding! We knew we had to come straight home."

"Just the two of us," said Sally. "We didn't want Grandfather, and as a matter of fact he didn't want to come. He was so dreadfully ashamed, poor old silly, because of the mess he'd got us into. We didn't tell him the real reason why we wanted to come home. We said we thought we ought to go to school or we'd never pass any examinations. Which is true. We know much more than other children about a lot of things, but we're hopeless at things like math and Latin."

"We flew back," said Clive. "But it took a bit of arranging, and we only arrived in England ten days ago. We—"

Sally gave a sudden giggle.

"At this moment we're supposed to be staying with relations while schools are arranged for us. We've got a lot of relations. So we put them off by writing to all of them and saying we were stopping with one of the others, and we came straight down here."

"We had to keep it dark," said Clive, "because Grandfather told us we must stay away from Castlecombe. McDougal has the right to occupy it, and keep people out, although he can't call it his property till the end of the month. I don't understand all that legal business. Anyway—"

"But does that mean he's living here?" Jeremy asked.

"No. He lives in London. He's a financier in the City. But he comes down sometimes, and he's the one who gives the orders. He's got rid of all our keepers and gardeners, who'd been with us for years, and put in his own men, about twice as many of them. The only people he kept are Moggs and his wife—I suppose because he felt he had to have someone who knew their way about the house. But they're no help to us. Moggsie would do anything for money. Well, and so we came down here just over a week ago, with nothing but our rucksacks, to find the Casket and the Sword."

"When we got out at the station," said Sally, "we saw some people we used to know quite well. But we'd grown so much and got so brown that they didn't recognize us. It gave us an awfully queer feeling, as though we were invisible."

"Which is what we wanted to be," said Clive, "and what we have been ever since. But first we went to the main gate, just to see what would happen. There was a man there whom we didn't know, and who didn't know us, of course, and he told us to shove off and said there'd be trouble if he caught us hanging about. So we shoved off. It was rather what we'd expected. We knew plenty of ways of getting in. And we were just discussing which would be the best when Mickey Few came along in his van."

"Mickey's one of our oldest friends," said Sally. "He's an odd-job man, and his van's fitted up as a workshop. He does plumbing and electrics and engines and roofs and windows—in fact, anything that can be done with ordinary tools and one pair of hands. And he plays the accordion and makes up songs of his own."

"We should never have thought of looking for him," said Clive. "Although he belongs to these parts he doesn't live here. He can't bear to live anywhere. He's always traveling round the country in his van. He just happened to come along, and we got into the van and he gave us supper at his lodgings in Reddicombe. And we talked about Castlecombe, naturally, and the end of it was that we told him what we'd come to do, and he said at once that he'd help us. You couldn't have anyone better, from our point of view. It was wonderful luck meeting him like that."

"I think it was more than luck," said Sally. "I think it was a token. It was a sign that we were right to come. Mickey's one of the very few people who would have understood." She looked at Jeremy. "You can't understand either, not yet, because you haven't heard about the Casket and the Sword. It's the sort of story you don't like telling people, as a rule, because you know it's no use. They'll simply laugh. They think it's a fairy tale. Even the Palfreys have almost stopped believing it. But Mickey isn't like that."

"His father and his grandfather worked in Castlecombe," said Clive. "He's been in and out of the place all his life. That makes a difference. Well, when it was dark he drove us back here and we got over the wall with his collapsible ladder. We went to our cave. It's very well hidden, as you'll see. We found it accidentally years ago, and we kept it secret. We were pretty sure these newcomers wouldn't know about it. And that's where we've been living ever since."

"For over a week!" Jeremy said. "But what have you been doing all this time?"

"Making a plan, and getting ready to carry it out. Reconnoitering the ground, finding out how many people we've got against us, and what they're like—things of that sort, mostly. And puzzling over a mystery. The thing we don't understand is why the place is so heavily guarded. We're pretty sure the keepers don't know, either. They're just carrying out orders. It's this man McDougal. It's almost as though he knew the story of the Casket and the Sword, and believed it. That's what we don't understand."

"At first we thought it was going to be easy," Sally said. "When we explored the Park, the day after we got in, it seemed peaceful enough, although it was overgrown and neglected. A lot of animals were straying about that ought to be kept in pens, and there were dogs preying on them. It was all a bit jungle-ish, in fact; but we're used to jungles. We didn't worry. We spotted about half a dozen keepers, but they didn't seem to be worrying either—just riding casually round. But when we broke into the house that night, to start our search, we found things were different."

"You've seen the house," said Clive. "You know the size it is. There are scores of windows to break in through, and hundreds of hiding places. We know every corner of it, naturally, just as we know every bit of the Park. But when we got inside we found that there were still people about, although it was late. They seemed to be keeping watch. And what was even worse, a lot of the doors were locked. We couldn't go where we wanted. We had to give up the idea of searching until Mickey could make us some skeleton keys, and that's one of the things that has held us up. We realized that it was going to be a long job, and so we went along to the gun room to try and bag some twenty-twos, but it was locked. In the end we went up to our old playroom—the lock on that door has been smashed for years—and collected bows and catapults and a few other things we thought we might want, including the trumpets. And then when we were getting out we were spotted. A dog barked. Luckily it was a dark night, but we were jolly nearly caught on the open grassland round the house."

"It was really the trumpets that saved us," said Sally. "I hadn't seen the point of taking them, but they came in jolly handy. We separated when the keepers came after us, and Clive blew his trumpet to draw them his way. And after a minute I blew mine. It was quite funny. We could hear them blundering about in the dark, and shouting and arguing about which way to go, and so we got back into the woods without any trouble. They're such fools! And I think they were scared as well. Castlecombe's an old, old place, and there's something about the sound of trumpets in the dark—like an army! So that was the beginning of the trumpet game."

"Next day everything was different," Clive said. "They were patrolling the Park and searching for our hiding place. There were more dogs, and they put padlocks on all the doors in the wall. It was as though they'd been expecting something. And that's the strange thing. Why should McDougal have been expecting someone to break into Castlecombe, unless he knows the story of the Casket and the Sword, and really believes that they're there to be found? Anyway, after that there was no point in trying to pretend we weren't here. We've just gone on preparing to carry out our plan. The rain rather held things up, but except for that we've been out and about, scouting and spying and harassing them with trumpet calls at night. Flitting about the Park like ghosts!"

"The night Clive and Mickey rigged up this lookout post I kept watch at the edge of the woods," Sally said. "I heard keepers, and so I blew a warning call, and then nipped away under the trees. They came after me at once, until Clive drew them off. They hate the trumpets. They don't know what to make of them at all."

"It's been a lot of fun," said Clive softly. "It's been a wonderful game. But I think the game's over now. Listen!"

He was sitting upright. For a time the excitement of the story and the warmth and security of their bird's nest had caused them almost to forget the hunt, which in any case had moved away from them into the far distance. But now the baying of the hounds was growing louder.

They listened in silence. The hunt was certainly moving their way. The two little monkeys began to chatter and scold, and suddenly they leaped to the very top of the tree, and sat close together on a swaying branch, with their arms round each other.

The hunt drew nearer. Mingled with the voices of the hounds they presently heard the thud of horses' hoofs and the shouts of men. Clive was frowning.

"You can't see anything from here. I'm going lower. Don't move, you two."

He slipped out of the nest, and they saw him a minute later lying along an outflung branch far below them, his thin, wiry body stretched so straight that almost nothing of him could be seen from the ground.

The hunt came closer still, and Sally glanced at Jeremy, not frightened but looking puzzled, her face very intent. They stared downward, at first seeing nothing but leaves and the great spreading trunk of the tree. Then they caught a glimpse of something dark amid the greenery, a black shadow passing over the grass a hundred feet below.

Other shapes followed, tawny in color. The noise of the hounds was now almost deafening, rising from directly beneath them. But suddenly it changed. There was a sound of snarling, rising in pitch and becoming fierce and ugly. An extraordinary commotion had broken out round the foot of the tree, and Sally turned in astonishment to Jeremy.

"They're fighting! But bloodhounds don't—"

She broke off as they heard men's voices. The keepers on their horses had broken through the undergrowth into the clearing beneath the sycamore. They were shouting to one another, and in an instant everything was explained.

"It's the mastiff!"

"Look out—he'll kill that hound!"

"Shoot the brute!"

"Don't be a fool! Use your whip!"

They heard the crack of whips mingled with the tumult of the fight and the cursing of the men. They heard a dog's deep voice raised in a sudden cry of pain. And by degrees some sort of order was restored. They heard the men talking again.

"That's got rid of him! Let him go."

"So that's what the hounds have been following—another false trail! I said they wouldn't be any good."

"Well, we might as well be getting back. No point in hanging around here."

The men all seemed to have voices of the same kind, rough and harsh, and they talked without any particular accent, as though they might have come from anywhere. They went on talking as they rode off, cracking their whips and evidently driving the hounds ahead of them, and gradually the sounds died away.

Sally leaned over and called to Clive.

"Clive, was it Prince?"

"Of course."

"He must have come after us. But it can't have been his scent that the hounds were following. Bloodhounds don't trail animals."

"No. But those idiots seem to think they do, which is lucky for us. I can't see him now. I hope he hasn't run away."

"Call to him, Clive. He can't be far off. Oh, the darling! He must have remembered us, after all!"

"Come on down," said Clive. "We ought to be getting back to the cave."

Jeremy slung his shopping bag round his neck, and they scrambled down. When they reached the lower branches Clive said:

"You two wait here a minute."

He had uncoiled the rope. He tossed one end over the outflung branch, so that it hung loose with both ends touching the ground. Then he slid down it and called in a low, clear voice:

"Prince! Prince! Come here, Prince! Come here!"

And after a few moments Prince came. He walked into the clearing, stopped a few feet from Clive, and stood confronting him with his forelegs stiffly apart and his great head thrust forward, uttering a queer little sound that was neither a whine nor a growl.

Clive was standing quite still. He had stuffed his catapult into his hip pocket, and his hands were empty.

"Well, do you know me, Prince? Do you remember

me? You jolly well ought to!" His voice was steady and warm and friendly. "What are you going to do, Prince? Are you going to bite my head off, you whacking great dog?"

There was a pause. Suddenly Prince uttered a short, low bark and his tail began to wag.

"Shut up, fathead!" said Clive sharply. "Don't make such a row!"

He went up to him and laid his hands on either side of the proud black head.

So then it was all right. Sally and Jeremy slid down the rope, and when Sally had coiled it, and restored it to its hiding place beneath a bush, she went to Prince and put her arms round him, and he licked her face. Then Jeremy was introduced to him, and he raised a paw to shake hands.

Sally's eyes were very bright.

"We must take him with us," she said.

"Of course."

"You see, the song's beginning to work out," said Sally softly. "Brothers of the woods . . . First Jeremy and now Prince—two new ones in one day!"

Clive was frowning.

"It must have been our scent those hounds were following, after all," he said. "Mine, to be exact. I think I know how it happened. We'd better wade through the old mill-stream, Sal, on our way back to the cave."

CHAPTER 6

the story in the cave

SOME THREE QUARTERS OF A MILE FARTHER along the southern ridge, a little to the westward of the house, there was an old granite quarry from which stone had been cut to build some of the older parts of Castlecombe.

It had long ago fallen into disuse. Soil had drifted down into it from the crest of the ridge, and a dense tangle of trees and undergrowth now filled it, so that there was nothing to show that it had ever been a quarry. But if you were bold enough to force your way into this jungle, which contained a great many brambles, and to work round the edge, you would presently come to a fissure in the rock face about eighteen inches wide, so overhung with climbing plants that you might easily pass it without knowing it was there.

It was the entrance to a natural passage which quickly widened, and which, after twisting a little, entered a cavern like a huge penthouse about forty feet long and thirty feet wide, with a high, sloping ceiling encrusted with stalactites.

"There was probably a terrific earthquake back in the Stone Age," said Clive. "The tors came bubbling up and enormous boulders went bouncing about like tennis balls. It looks as though this was a solid mass of rock that got split up. The quarriers must have uncovered the entrance, but it was almost completely blocked when we found it. We had to dig our way in."

"We think they got scared," said Sally. "There's a legend, you see, that this is a bad place, although nobody knows why. We think they thought there was an evil presence lurking in the cave, and that's why they didn't quarry any more."

But the only presence lurking there when they entered was a small elderly man in shirt sleeves and a bowler hat. He was sitting cross-legged on the ground by the light of two hurricane lamps, holding an accordion in his hands and keeping an eye on a structure of stones and old biscuit tins over which a pot was simmering. Clive had given a call as they entered, and he turned his head to greet them with a quick, sudden movement like that of a small bird. His eyes twinkled. At the sight of Prince he said:

"Hullo—'ullo!"

Prince was not happy at that moment. He had not liked the look of the entrance to the cave. Clive had had to pull him, and Sally had pushed, and he had come reluctantly along the dark, twisting passage, growling and protesting, but always gently, in a way which made it clear that he accepted them as his friends and masters, no matter what they did. He now stood looking at the little man, with the hair on his back beginning to rise.

The little man seemed quite unperturbed.

"Come to join the regiment, have you, my dear? I hope you'll attend to your own victuals. You're a mortal big mouth to feed."

"It's Prince," said Sally. "You ought to remember him, Mickey. Prince, where are your manners? Don't you know your friends?"

Perhaps Prince did know, or perhaps he was reassured by the little man's gay, chirruping voice, with its touch of West Country brogue. He drew closer and raised a paw, and they shook hands.

"And this is Jeremy, the boy we told you about. He got in under the river barrier. He's jolly good."

"Looks all right," said Mickey Few, with a friendly nod to Jeremy. "A bit like me at that age, only not so fierce. Cor! Like a roarin' lion, I was!"

"Well, here's a rabbit for you," said Clive, handing it to him with a grin. He had killed it with his catapult as they came along, and pouched it on the spot with his hunting knife. "I say, Mickey, they're using bloodhounds now! Did you hear?"

"Bloodhounds!" Mickey Few looked up sharply. "I thought I heard something as I was on my way here, but once you get inside it's like being in a tomb. Bloodhounds, eh? That's bad."

"Yes," said Clive. "They came to the sycamore. Luckily

Prince got tangled up with them, and the keepers thought it was his trail the hounds were following—which shows you how much they know about bloodhounds! But I'm afraid they were really after me. I cut my knee the other day and tied a handkerchief round it. It may have come off without my noticing. If the keepers found it, that's just what they'd need to give the hounds my scent. The trouble is, we shall have them nosing round here sooner or later, particularly if the weather keeps fine."

"It's lucky they didn't think of it before," said Mickey. "The sooner you get your business over, the better, my dear. Well, everything's ready now. I've finished the keys and I've done the fuses, and I got the fireworks this morning—there's the parcel over there. They had to be ordered from the factory. The shops don't stock 'em at this time of year."

"Oh, good!" said Clive, and went eagerly to examine the parcel. "Oh, that's grand! We'll go in tonight, Mickey. It'll be much easier now Jeremy's here."

Jeremy did not understand this, but he was content to wait until they told him. At the moment he was examining the cave.

Its only furnishings were a few flat stones and ledges of rock which served as tables and shelves. The floor was strewn with rushes and dried bracken, like a dwelling in the Middle Ages, and there were heaps of the same stuff covered with waterproof sheets and blankets to make litters for sitting and sleeping on. But bare and somber though it was, the cave was given a homey aspect by the many things it contained—things for cooking and washing, tins of food, a pitcher of water and a drum of oil, tools and garments, a big unstrung bow, which was Clive's, and, resting on one of the ledges, two silver trumpets with red tassels, so polished that they gleamed softly in the light of the lamps.

All the things from outside had been brought in by Mickey. He left his van hidden in a copse some distance from the Park and came in over the wall with his ladder, generally after dark, but sometimes in broad daylight, as he had done that morning. Until the coming of the bloodhounds there had not been much risk. However much they galloped round, the keepers could not possibly watch all the fifteen miles of wall.

The cave was very tidy, and as clean as could be expected. The Palfreys, like Mickey, had the knack of making a home for themselves wherever they were. Jeremy listened to them excitedly discussing the fireworks.

"Two rockets," said Clive. "Ten flares, and about a hundred squibs and bangers—good big ones, some of them. Well, that ought to do the job all right! I must say, I envy you and Jeremy, Sal!" He came and sat down on one of the litters. "What's for dinner, Mick? I'm half starving, although we did have some sandwiches."

"It's a sort of hot pot," said Mickey. "Odds and ends and bits and pieces. But you'll have to wait a few more minutes. These spirit cookers are a slow job. Matter of fact, I was just tuning up to give myself a song when you came in."

"Well, give us all one," said Sally, sitting down and pulling Jeremy down beside her. "Sing Jeremy your advertising song."

"Well, I might, mightn't I? He might turn into a customer." Mickey winked at Jeremy. "You see, I'm a handyman, my dear, and I have to advertise like anyone else. Some folks put pieces in the paper and others has their names up in lights, but I do it with a song."

He picked up his accordion and sang:

"I'll mend your pots and pans,
I'll patch your boots and shoes;
I'll mow the lawn and light the fires
And paint the fence and pump the tires—
Service with a smile, ma'am!
Anything I can do
I'll do in a tick, and they call me Mick—
Mick Montgomery Few!

"I'll fix the leaky tap,
I'll make the engine go;
I'll mend the roof and chop the wood
And spank the kids to make them good—
Everything fair and square, ma'am,
Honest and straight and true,
And done in a tick, and they call me Mick—
Mick Montgomery Few.

"I'll make the chimney draw,
I'll bake a cake for tea;
I'll beat the rugs and sweep the stairs,

Or pull your teeth or cut your hairs.
Never you mind the fee, ma'am,
It's only a bob to you!
And done in a tick, and they call me Mick—
Mick Montgomery Few.

"I'll spin you out a yarn
To make you laugh or cry;
I'll read the cards to tell your chance,
Or play a tune to make you dance.
Leave it all to me, ma'am,
Nobody else will do!
I'm quick as a lick and they call me Mick—
Mick Montgomery Few!"

The tune was so gay and lively that it had Jeremy jigging up and down on his seat. When he had finished singing Mickey started to do a little dance, but he had to stop because the excitement was too much for Prince, who jumped up and started barking at the top of his voice. Clive was laughing.

"That song's a swindle," he said. "His name isn't really Montgomery. He just put that in for swank. And he charges much more than a bob, and I bet he's never pulled a tooth in his life!"

"I'll start on yours if you aren't careful," said Mickey, rolling his eyes ferociously. "I'll have the lot of 'em—one by one! It's your turn now, Miss Sal. What are you going to give us?"

"How about 'Daffydowndilly'? Do you think you can manage the tune?" Sally asked.

"I can try. You sing, and I'll follow."

So Sally sang in her clear, birdlike voice:

"Daffydowndilly
My lady will come
Down by the grass walk
To welcome me home,
Gay as a gillyvor,
Fresh as the may,
And spring shall strew blossoms
To brighten her way.

"Daffydowndilly
On Daffodil Down—
Sweetest of ladies
And ever my own!

"Daffydowndilly
I'll bring from the fair
Ribbons and buckles
And combs for her hair,
Comfits and lavender
For her delight,
And a song for the morning,
A kiss for the night.

"Daffydowndilly
On Daffodil Down—
Most lovely of ladies,
And I am her own!"

When it was over she looked half shyly at Jeremy. "That isn't the only Daffydowndilly song," she said.

"It's just our private one. There's a part of our garden that's still called Daffodil Down—a sort of hillock, with a grass walk and some old pear trees and great banks of daffodils in the spring. I never go there without thinking of the lady, light as a feather, hurrying over the grass—almost dancing—to see what he's brought her from the fair!"

"But do you mean to say you made it up?" asked Jeremy, rather puzzled.

"Heavens, no! It was one of our ancestors. 'Gillyvor' is an old country name for wallflower, and 'comfits' were sugar plums. It may be very old."

"We've got a lot of songs in our family," Clive said. "People have made them up at one time or another, and we learn them and pass them on. But they've never been written down, so nobody knows them except us."

"It's singing songs that matters," said Mickey. "Having them in your head, handy for when you want them. Well, we'll have the 'Trumpet Song,' just to be sure it hasn't gone astray, and then we'll have some grub."

When the meal was over the Palfreys lay down and promptly went to sleep, because, as Clive said, they expected to be pretty busy during the night. Jeremy tried to do the same, but the strangeness of everything made it difficult. Besides, he had now learned what the fireworks were for, and the part he was to play in the plan for that night; and the prospect was exciting enough to keep anyone awake. There was something else as well—a troublesome thought at the back of his mind, like a person tugging at his sleeve. But in spite of it all he dropped off in the end, with the words of the "Trumpet Song" ringing in his head—"We must fight and conquer; we must do or die! . . ."

He awoke in a dead silence and sat up with a jerk, thinking he was all alone. Perhaps it would not have surprised him very much to find that the cave had vanished, and Clive and Sally with it, and the whole of Castlecombe. But Sally was there, seated between the two lamps with a book on her knee and a stub of pencil in her hand. Prince lay asleep on the ground beside her.

"Hullo!" she said, smiling at him. "You've had a long sleep. I'm so glad."

"Where are the others?"

"Mickey has gone to set up his flares along the ridge and fix the fuses. It's easier to do by daylight, although of course he'll have to go back and light them after dark. And Clive has gone to the sycamore to see if anything's happening round the house, and if the hounds are out again. They ought both to be back soon. It's nearly supper-time. Would you like some tea?"

"Lemonade would do," said Jeremy, "if there's still some left."

Sally got up to get it for him, and Jeremy thought of the calm way in which she had mentioned the bloodhounds. But then he thought that she was quite right.

They couldn't just sit there doing nothing because of a few hounds; and Clive could certainly look after himself. She handed him a picnic cup.

"What have you been doing?" Jeremy asked.

"Drawing a map. It'll make it easier for you to understand. Come here and I'll show you."

Jeremy sat beside her. She had drawn a rough oval on the end page of the book, representing the wall of the Park, and inside it she had marked the ridges and the woods, the river, and the house with its gardens, surrounded by open ground, with the five great avenues running out like the spokes of a wheel. She pointed with a rough, firm forefinger.

"Here's where we are, and here's where you and I have to go tonight. It's a tor, a huge rock which is known as the Stooping Lady, because that's rather what it looks like. It overhangs the King's Vista—there—running from the house to the Bird Lake. That's the shortest and broadest of the avenues, only about a half a mile long. They used to hold jousts there in the old days, but now it's where the cattle mostly spend the night, after drinking in the lake. There are generally one or two keepers about, partly to stop them being worried by the dogs. Well, we climb up onto the Stooping Lady. She's very steep in front, but there's a fairly easy way up over her back; and there's a sort of hollow between her shoulders and her head—the nape of her neck, as you might say—where we can hide and see what's going on. We stay there and wait for the rocket."

"Yes," said Jeremy, poring over the map and thinking how vast the Park was, and how much of it he had still to see.

He already knew roughly what the plan was. The idea was to draw as many keepers as possible away from the house, because it was so closely guarded since the Palfreys had broken in that something special had to be done if they were to have any chance of getting in again.

The rocket, which Mickey would send up when Clive and he were ready, was to be a signal to Sally and Jeremy to start letting off firecrackers along the King's Vista, stampeding the cattle, and causing as much noise and confusion as possible. Mickey would have already lighted the slow-burning fuses on his flares, and if they worked as they were intended to do they would start breaking out along the ridge, looking like the lights of an invading army, or as though the woods were on fire (there was some danger of a real fire being started, but in view of the recent rains it was not very great). This would be something else to alarm and distract the keepers—firecrackers and stampeding cattle in one direction and flares in another! And while they were galloping frantically in all directions, trying to find out what was happening, Clive and Mickey would hurry round to the other side of the house and break in.

"Yes," said Jeremy, thinking it over. "Yes, I see. It's jolly clever. But what will you and I do when we've let off our bangers and stampeded the cattle?"

"Well, it depends. It's no use trying to plan too far

ahead. So many things can happen, and you can't expect everything to go exactly right. The best thing would be if we could get into the house, too. Clive's going to leave a window unfastened, and we've arranged where we'd meet inside. Then I'd stay with him. The house is so huge. We can hide there for days, if we have to. And if possible you and Mickey would go back to the cave."

"Oh," said Jeremy, looking up. "But—"

"But it probably won't happen. They're going to break in the menagerie side, which means that we'd have a long way to go, and we'd have to cross the King's Vista, which might be very risky. There's no cover, as you can see. Most likely we shall have to hide in the woods until the excitement has died down, and then get back to the cave. And Mickey will come to the cave, too, as soon as he can."

"Leaving Clive in the house alone? But why will Mickey come back?"

"Because he's only going in to attend to the locked doors. He's got to show Clive how to work the skeleton keys and to pick any locks that they won't open. He's a very good locksmith. But he can't help to find the Casket and the Sword. Only the Palfreys can do that."

"Oh," said Jeremy again.

"Clive and I hoped we'd be able to do it together, but if we can't Clive will have to do it himself. It must be him, because all Castlecombe may belong to him someday."

"Because he's going to be the earl?"

Sally nodded.

"But anyway I couldn't do it. It's not just a matter of finding them. The Casket will have to be smuggled out of the house, which isn't going to be easy. But Clive will find a way. He's so clever. He can do anything."

"Yes," said Jeremy.

He was suddenly unhappy. Clive was so clever, and Sally, too; and they were Palfreys, and he was just a stranger who was giving them a little help. He felt that he was being left out.

He said rather dolefully after a silence:

"You know, you haven't told me yet. You keep on talking about the Casket and the Sword, but you haven't explained."

"Oh, poor Jeremy!" Sally cried.

She touched his hand with a little friendly movement.

"It's because we're shy," she said. "It's such a queer story, and scarcely anyone believes it. And there's a part we'd never told a soul until we told Mickey the other day. But it isn't fair, is it? You've a right to be told—particularly as your name's Jeremy."

She sat considering for a moment.

"Have you heard of the Brothers of the Coast?"

"The buccaneers?" said Jeremy. "I've read about them. They raided treasure ships in the Caribbean."

"Yes. The chief one was Henry Morgan. He reformed in the end, and became governor of Jamaica, I think, and Charles the Second knighted him. But when he was still being a buccaneer an ancestor of ours was one of his lieutenants. He was one of the roving Palfreys, and his name was Jeremy, too—Jeremy Palfrey. Well, he was badly wounded in a sea battle, and when he knew he hadn't long to live he came back to Castlecombe to die, which is what the Palfreys always do if they can, even the bad ones. He brought a great oak chest with him, and everyone thought it must be full of loot. But no one knew what was inside it, because he always kept it locked.

"He only lived a month or two after he came home. He behaved very strangely, scarcely speaking to anyone. He wandered about the house, particularly at night. He was like a lost soul, straying through the rooms and corridors as though he were searching for something, but he never said what he was doing.

"When he died he left a will behind him, which the lawyers still have. It was a sort of prophecy. It said that a time would come when the house of Castlecombe would be in danger of falling into the hands of 'a stranger, yet not strange.' Those were the actual words. And it said that when this happened the Palfreys must search for the Casket and the Sword, which were hidden in a secret place. Only a Palfrey could find them; but only if they believed in them, and if they were both old and young. I forget exactly how it went, but it was all in riddles, you see.

"No one could make head or tail of it. There were a few statuettes and ornaments in old Jeremy's chest, souvenirs that he'd picked up, but nothing specially valuable and nothing that gave a clue. They thought that when he'd gone prowling about the house he might have been arranging a hiding place for this Casket and Sword he talked about, but although the family searched for a long time they never found anything. In the end they decided that his wits had been wandering, and that there was nothing to be found.

"It didn't seem to matter. This was soon after the Restoration, and the Palfreys were enormously rich and powerful. No one dreamed that the house could ever fall into a stranger's hands. So the whole thing was more or less forgotten. It became a family legend, and no one believed that there were really and truly a Casket and a Sword."

Sally was silent for a moment, and Jeremy said:

"But you and Clive believe it?"

"Yes," said Sally. "It was Clive who made us both believe it. Grandfather told us the story, with all the other family stories, when we were both quite small. But afterward Clive wrote down a solemn vow that we would always believe it, no matter what happened, and that if the need arose we would search until we found the Casket and the Sword. We pricked our fingers and signed the paper with our blood, and after that we never had the slightest trouble in believing it. But now we come to the really strange part, which we've never told, except to Mickey. Jeremy, do you believe in ghosts?"

"No," said Jeremy. "At least, I don't think I do."

"We do. It isn't a matter of seeing or hearing them. If you live in a very old house, where your ancestors have lived for hundreds of years, you can't help having a feeling

that in a sort of way they're still there. It isn't a thing you worry about—it's just the family. Well, what happened was this.

"It was about four years ago, before there was any trouble, or anyway before Clive and I knew about it. I was nearly nine, and Clive was eleven. I woke up suddenly one night with the moonlight streaming into my room. I had a feeling that someone had called to me, and I thought it must be Clive, who was next door. So I got up and went out into the passage, and at exactly the same moment Clive's door opened and he came out, too.

"There was a queer flickering little light at the far end of the passage. It was a rushlight, I think, like they used in the old days. A man was holding it. We could only see his head and shoulders. He had a bandage round his head and a patch over one eye. We knew at once that it was our great-great-great-great-cousin, Jeremy Palfrey.

"He didn't say anything. He smiled and beckoned to us to follow him, and we did. We went along dark corridors, and up and down stairways, and through doorways and across rooms, following that little flickering light. It was very queer. Presently we seemed to go through a wall. There was a little wooden staircase and a thick door and then we were in a tiny room that we'd never seen before. It was like a prison cell, with no window. There were rushes on the floor, and a low table, and a wooden stool and a narrow wooden bed and an earthenware pitcher of water. That's all I can remember. But there was a big black beam across the ceiling, so low that Cousin Jeremy could touch it easily. He reached up and did something, I don't know what, and then he pushed, and part of the beam moved and uncovered a hole. He held up the light, and we got on the table and looked in. Standing on the rafters was a golden casket about a foot long, of a queer old design, with six feet shaped like claws. It wasn't dusty or anything. It shone as though it had been newly polished. And lying beside it was a great curved sword in a scabbard, with a big handle—a pirate's boarding cutlass.

"We looked, but we knew that we mustn't touch. We got down again, and Cousin Jeremy moved the beam and hid the hole. Then he smiled at us. All this time no one had spoken a word or made a sound, but we knew exactly what he meant. He was saying, 'There they are, when the time comes! . . .' And then we went back along the passages, until Cousin Jeremy seemed suddenly to vanish. We found that we were outside our rooms, and we went back to bed, still without saying a word."

Sally was again silent for a few moments. She looked at Jeremy with a smile.

"Of course, you think it was just a dream."

"Yes," said Jeremy.

"So did I, when I woke up—until I told Clive. But you see, he'd had exactly the same dream!"

"Oh." Jeremy sat in silence, feeling rather queer. At length he asked: "Did you go back to that room?"

"We couldn't find it. We thought it ought to be fairly easy. It was bound to be somewhere in the older parts of the house, because not all of it had been built in Cousin Jeremy's day. We thought we knew all the secrets. There's a priest's niche, for instance, up one of the chimneys, which goes back to anti-papist times, when the priests were on the run. The family was Catholic then. And there are one or two old, secret passages which aren't secret any more. But this was nothing like anything that we knew about, and—well, we couldn't find it, that's all."

Jeremy wrinkled his forehead.

"But then—"

"It was like something you know but can't quite remember at the moment—like a word you've got on the tip of your tongue. And we decided that we weren't meant to remember. The time hadn't come. So we stopped fussing about it. We didn't worry even when Grandfather told us that we were broke and going to Africa. He didn't say anything about McDougal, or the risk of losing Castlecombe. But when he did tell us that Castlecombe was in danger we looked at one another and we knew instantly that this was the time. We knew we had to come home."

"Yes, I see. But have you remembered yet where the room is?"

"No," said Sally slowly. "Not yet. We thought we should when we broke into the house. We thought it would suddenly come back to us—or anyway that something would happen. But it wasn't like that. The house didn't give us any help. It was cold and dead and locked up. We felt as though it were angry with us for having left it in the hands of strangers. There were people moving about whose names and faces we didn't know. Oh, it was dreadful! I've never been so miserable in my life as I was just then. But afterward everything was changed in a flash. That was when Clive played the trumpet call. . . .

"I didn't want to bother with the trumpets. We had so many things to carry. But Clive seemed to know. Oh, it was so wonderful, hearing that call in the dark, and the silly keepers dashing after it! It was so marvelous! It was like a challenge! It was as though Castlecombe had come to life again! There's always something wonderful about a trumpet. They're ages old, but they always sound young. It was like an answer to the prophecy, you see. And then I felt quite sure we should find the room and the Casket. Oh, Jeremy, do you understand?"

"Yes," said Jeremy, "I do understand. I felt just the

same when I heard the trumpet. That's why I felt I had to answer. That's why I'm here!"

Then they sat looking at one another with their eyes shining, and no more to be said, as though they had been friends and companions for a hundred years. Everything was explained, now; everything was clear and understood. The great dog, Prince, had awakened and was lying crouched in front of them with his head raised, as though he, too, had been listening to the story. But after a silence Jeremy returned to the thought that had been at the back of his mind for a long time, like a person tugging at his sleeve.

"There's just one thing I'm worrying about," he said. "Aunt Eleanor—"

His voice was drowned as Prince's sudden barking filled the cave. Clive's voice sounded from the entrance, and he came in saying:

"All right, all right, all right! It's only me!"

He had taken his bow, and he carried a dead kid over his shoulder.

"More food, if wanted. Anyway, I thought a trail of fresh blood might puzzle the hounds by covering my scent. I'm not sure if it will work, but goats smell pretty strong when they're alive!"

"Were the hounds out?" Sally asked.

"Not a sign of them. Having a nice rest, I expect, after this morning. But something did happen, Sal."

"What?"

"A whacking great car, a Bentley Continental. It drove up to the house about half an hour ago."

"Who was in it?"

"A man nearly as big as the car, in a tweed suit. I just got a glimpse of him while he was walking about outside with one of the keepers. He looked like a prize fighter, except that he had gray hair."

"McDougal!" said Sally.

"I expect so. Perhaps he's come to take charge because I plugged that keeper. There'd have been just time for him to drive down from London, if they rang up. So that makes it jolly interesting! Hasn't Mickey finished those flares yet? When are we going to have supper? I'm hungry again."

CHAPTER 7

the battle in the dusk

THE ARRIVAL OF MUNGO McDOUGAL seemed in a way to change everything, although for practical purposes it changed nothing. It filled the air with an electric feeling, causing them all to tighten their muscles as they realized that the climax was upon them and that now the battle had truly begun. On the other hand, it made it more than ever necessary to go ahead with their plan, because any delay would enable McDougal to take further precautions which might make it even more difficult to get into the house.

But there was Aunt Eleanor. Since Jeremy would not be going back to the cottage that night, a message must be sent, tied to an arrow; and Clive must shoot the arrow, since he knew the exact spot. Clive wanted at first to go alone, leaving Sally and Jeremy to get as much rest as possible before the night's work; but Jeremy asked to be allowed to go with him. He thought it very likely that Aunt Eleanor would be waiting on the hillock, wondering and worrying. In that case he might have a chance to call to her over the wall, as Clive had done, and when she heard his voice she would know that he was really all right. The truth is, Jeremy was rather conscience-stricken about Aunt Eleanor.

This meant that the plan had to be changed a little. Instead of going straight to the Stooping Lady with Sally, Jeremy would leave earlier with Clive, who would guide him to the tor after shooting the arrow. Clive would then return to the cave to join forces with Mickey, when he came back from lighting the flares. In the meantime Sally would have started for the tor, waiting until it was dark enough for her to come the shortest way, across the open spaces instead of round under the cover of the woods. These movements had to be carefully planned, and Clive set his wrist watch by Mickey's big silver pocket watch to make sure that they were the same.

The sun was setting when the two boys left the cave. The perfect day was sinking into a perfect twilight, bathed in a warm red glow sweeping across the sky from the west. Everything was still at that moment, with no breeze stirring (no keeper either, so far as they could tell), and scarcely a sound of birds or animals, as though the Park and all its creatures were waiting in a long pause for the passing of the day and the coming of the night.

Clive led the way out of the quarry and up toward the crest of the ridge, keeping as usual to the parts where the trees were thickest. Although he had had very little rest, he seemed as fresh as ever, springy on his feet and very alert, with a tight look about his mouth.

"No need to hurry," he said. "We've plenty of time, and we shall probably get all the running we want later on." He grinned at Jeremy. "The lull before the storm!"

He was carrying his long bow, with a quiver of arrows hanging at his side. His catapult was stuffed into his belt, and his silver trumpet was tied across his shoulders so that it did not bang about. Jeremy carried no weapons except his knife and a stout, knobby stick which Mickey had cut for him; but he had Aunt Eleanor's shopping bag, containing fireworks, matches, and several lengths of slow-burning fuse, slung over his shoulder. He also had a small electric torch.

They went at a steady walk, talking in low undertones, partly as a precaution, but also, perhaps, because the warm tranquillity of the evening was something they did not like to disturb. It was hard to believe in battles at that moment. The hush so filled the air that even the snapping of a twig was like a small explosion, and Jeremy could hear the sound of Clive's steady breathing and feel the beating of his own heart.

His heart nearly jumped out of his mouth when he heard a sudden rustle in the bushes close behind them; and then Prince appeared, and came up to them wagging his tail. Clive frowned slightly.

"I suppose the old boy was restless, so Sally thought she'd better let him go. I really wanted him to go with her, to keep other dogs off."

"We haven't heard any dogs," Jeremy said.

"No. They're probably all still asleep. You'll hear

them later on. But as a matter of fact, you don't get them so much toward the center of the Park. The keepers drive them off, and anyway there's better hunting up on the ridges. Sal will probably be all right."

"I wonder if they'll bring the bloodhounds out?"

"Well, if they do they'll be after me," said Clive, and he grinned again.

They went on their way with the great dog following silently at their heels. The shadows were lengthening. Jeremy caught a sudden glimpse in the distance of a stone building, flanked by trees, which made him think of the pictures of Greek temples he had seen in books.

"That's what it's meant to be," said Clive, when he told him this. "It's at the end of one of the avenues, called the Greek Vista, which runs almost due south from the house. The trees are cypresses."

"But what's it for?" asked Jeremy.

"Nothing special. Just something to look at. It was built in George the Third's reign."

As the twilight deepened the evening grew less silent. There were movements in the undergrowth, small stirrings, little squeaks and flurries as the smaller creatures of the Park returned to life. And suddenly there was a great commotion as a large animal went crashing off through the bushes only a few yards away.

"A moose," said Clive, with a chuckle at Jeremy's startled face. "They live on the trees. One has to watch out for those beauties. A bull moose will charge sometimes."

They emerged presently onto a bridle path and followed it for several hundred yards, keeping close to the edge so that they could take cover if they heard the sound of horses. But there was no sign of activity yet on the part of the keepers, and after leaving the path they passed over the crest of the ridge and went down the other side toward the wall.

"We're almost there," said Clive. "I want to shoot from the same tree as last night. It gave me a good view of the hillock, and we'll know exactly where we are. This way."

A minute later they reached the tree, an old oak with low branches that made it easy to climb. Jeremy started up while Clive paused to talk to Prince, putting a hand on either side of his head while he murmured in his ear:

"You're to stay here and keep watch. On guard, Prince! Don't move!"

Then he followed Jeremy, and looking down they saw Prince lying at the foot of the tree with his head raised and his ears cocked.

The oak was not very tall, but it was on higher ground than the wall and near enough to it to enable them to get a wide view of the world outside. The wall was the first thing Jeremy saw as he peered through a gap in the leaves to get his bearings. It rose up about twenty yards away, its upper part still faintly pink in the fast-dying light. Beyond it was the river, invisible from where they were, and on the far side the land rose, gently at first and then more steeply, mounting the ridge beyond which lay Aunt Eleanor's cottage, less than half a mile away. And in the foreground was Jeremy's hillock, with its single tree.

"I said the arrow would be sticking in it, or very near it," he murmured. "Do you think you can score a direct hit?"

Clive was fishing in his quiver for the right arrow, the one to which Jeremy's message was tightly tied with thread.

"I'll try, but I can't promise. This bow has a thirty-pound draw. It's awkward to handle if you can't get a proper stance."

He shifted about, trying to find the best position. A cow lowed in the distance, just as it had done the night before, and a bird twittered drowsily. A dark shape flashed silently through the dusk, and Jeremy thought it must have been a bat. The tree and the top of the hillock stood out clearly above a pool of shadow, catching the last gleams of the sunset. And the night before Jeremy had stood there, visible to Clive but seeing only darkness. Now he was part of the darkness! To gaze over the little valley gave him a queer feeling, as though he had gone a very long way and were looking back from a distance to the place he had left behind.

Suddenly he made a movement.

"Wait! Don't shoot yet!"

He had seen what he had hoped for and had half expected. Something moved in the shadow at the foot of the hillock. A tall, slim figure strode up the slope, becoming more visible as it reached the crest. It was not hard to recognize Aunt Eleanor, even in that light. She stood by the tree, staring toward the wall.

"Jeremy! Are you anywhere near? Can you hear me?"

Jeremy glanced at Clive, who nodded.

"Not too loud. Don't say too much."

"I'm here, Aunt Eleanor," Jeremy called. "I'm absolutely all right, but I can't talk. There's an arrow coming."

Clive let the arrow go, altering his aim to avoid the risk of hitting her. It landed about three yards from her, and they saw her move swiftly and bend down to pluck it out of the earth. Jeremy wondered if she had thought of bringing matches or a torch so that she could read it. He hadn't written very much—only that he had something very important to do, and would be staying in the Park that night and would try to let her have more news in the morning.

Then something rather puzzling happened. After picking up the arrow Aunt Eleanor said something with her face turned away from them, speaking in her normal voice so that they could not hear the words. She seemed to be talking to some other person standing at the foot of the hillock, hidden from them in the shadow. Then she turned toward them again and called:

"Jeremy—"

But that was all they heard. At this moment Prince began to bark.

The dog's deep, baying voice shattered the silence like a clap of thunder, causing Jeremy to start violently and setting up an instant commotion in the woods around them, a twitter of startled birds, a scurry of life in the undergrowth. But there was more than this. Two large bodies, it seemed, were plunging about in the bushes near the foot of the tree. Mingled with Prince's furious barking was the voice of some other creature, raised in a savage, grunting squeal.

"We must go down!" Clive exclaimed.

He slid past Jeremy, dropping from branch to branch with the agility he always showed, and Jeremy followed as quickly as he could, bewildered by the ferocity of this tumult that now filled the darkness. Prince's bark had become an ugly growl, deep in his throat—the same sound that they had heard that morning when they came upon him tearing up the body of a fawn. It sounded like a fight to the death, and as Jeremy reached the lower branches Clive said sharply:

"Don't come any farther! Get out your torch!"

He had spoken just too late. Jeremy lost his foothold at that moment, felt a dead branch snap as his hand clutched it, grabbed in vain for another, bounced on the lowest branch of all, and finally landed on his back at the foot of the tree. He was up in an instant, not badly hurt but badly shaken. Feeling sick and giddy, with the wind knocked out of him, he stood helplessly with his back to the trunk of the tree.

Not more than five yards away two powerful forms were writhing and twisting with a furious energy in the shadows. Jeremy could faintly distinguish the big, black form of Prince grappling in ferocious combat with some lighter-colored animal that seemed smaller but no less deadly. They were rolling over and over in a flurry of legs and bodies, amid a hideous din of grunting and snarling, and they were coming closer to Jeremy.

He stood staring at them, still dazed by his fall, as though this were one of those dreams in which one watches the approach of danger and cannot run. The dim half-light lent the writhing forms a nightmarish quality, monstrous and terrifying. Jeremy thought of his stick, which he had lost in his fall, and instinctively bent down to try to find it. At this moment Clive called from the branch immediately above him:

"Jeremy, what are you playing at? Pull yourself together! Get behind the tree and shine your torch on them! Go on, *do it!*"

The last words were snapped out like an order given on the parade ground, and they brought back Jeremy's wits. Obeying instantly, he dodged behind the tree, pulling the torch out of his pocket; and peering round the trunk he shone it on the two struggling animals.

He had a glimpse of tusks, and realized that the beast Prince was fighting was a wild boar. There was a momentary pause. The sudden bright beam of light had the effect Clive had been counting on. It did what no amount of violence could have done, causing both animals to hesitate in an instant of astonishment.

Jeremy saw that Prince was lying half on his back, his teeth gripping the tough skin at the side of the boar's neck and his great paws thrusting it away, while the boar, standing over him, was seeking to bury its tusks in his body. Things happened very quickly. The pause was only

a matter of seconds, but this was all Clive needed. Jeremy heard the twang of the bowstring, and then there was an arrow sticking out of thc boar's side, just behind the shoulder blade.

For a moment it seemed to have had no effect. The boar, still full of fight, seemed to be trying to wrench itself away from Prince in order to turn upon this new attacker. Jeremy saw its eyes flash golden in the light of the torch as its head swung round. It looked straight toward him, but it was already weakening. Suddenly Prince heaved himself to his feet, and bringing all the weight of his body to bear upon it, thrust it over on its side.

Clive dropped down from the tree and came and put his arm round Jeremy's shoulders.

"Are you all right?"

"Yes," said Jeremy, although he was trembling. "It was the bump, that's all. I'm all right now."

"You nearly gave me heart failure!" said Clive. "Keep your torch on them. He might revive. They're tough, boars are, and that's a jolly big one."

"Would Prince have been able to kill him?"

"No fear! He'd have killed Prince, if anything. No dog can fight a boar single-handed—precious few other animals either."

The boar was still fighting, but its struggles were dying down, and presently Prince was able to bury his teeth in its throat. When it was all over Clive got out his own torch and went to where the great dog stood with its flanks heaving and blood running from its jowls. He talked in a quiet, friendly voice.

"Let's have a look at you, old boy. Quiet, Prince—steady!"

Jeremy came round the tree and shone his torch on the ground to find his stick. The grass was littered with fireworks that had fallen out of his bag, and he started to retrieve them.

"It might be worse," said Clive. "He's been ripped on the chest and shoulder, but I don't think the tusks really went into him. The sooner I can get him back to the cave and clean him up, the better."

"You've got to take me to the Stooping Lady first," Jeremy said.

"I know." Clive was looking at the dead boar. "A whopper!" he murmured. "The old man of the family. I wonder if his lair's somewhere near. If there's a sow with a farrow she'd be even more dangerous."

He bent down and tried to pull the arrow out of the carcass, but it was so deeply embedded that he could not shift it. And then he straightened himself and stood listening. They heard the distant sound of a police whistle, and then horses' hoofs, growing more distinct. Two or more keepers were coming in their direction along the broad ride that encircled the Park, running beside the wall.

Clive switched off his torch.

"We'd better get moving," he said. "But don't leave any of those bangers behind."

Jeremy was beginning to understand the rules of the game of hide-and-seek which the Palfreys played with the keepers by day and by night, always with the advantage that they had known the Park all their lives. It was the keeper on foot you had to watch out for, the one who stayed still, waiting and listening, behind a bush or up a tree. The ones on the move were easy, particularly those on horseback; you slipped away when you heard them coming. You could sound a trumpet call and be a hundred yards from the spot before anyone could reach it. You could use a torch under the trees provided you flicked it on and off quickly and kept moving. But there was a certain danger in this. The keepers carried shotguns. So far they had never used them except occasionally to drive dogs away from the open spaces where the cattle grazed. But after what Clive had done to one of them that morning they might be inclined to shoot at any light they saw. It was a risk that had to be borne in mind.

Jeremy hastily gathered up the last of the fireworks, still using his torch, but keeping it close to the ground so that the beam should not travel. He had found his stick. They climbed rapidly up the ridge, following as straight a line as the ground permitted, Clive leading, with Prince running at his side, limping a little, and Jeremy close behind.

They heard the voices of men behind them, but these grew fainter. After passing over the crest of the ridge they slowed to a walk again. It was now very dark, with only the faintest glimmer of dusk still lingering in the sky and the stars already showing. The moon would not be up for nearly another hour. Then they heard a police whistle again, and Clive gave a little grunt.

"They use those things to keep in touch after dark. Perhaps those chaps have found the boar. They'll probably spot the arrow, although I broke the end off, so they'll know we've been there. It doesn't much matter. By the way, there was someone with your aunt just now. Did you see?"

Jeremy was startled. In the flurry of events he had forgotten all about Aunt Eleanor. She, too, must have heard the sounds of the fight.

"I thought she turned and spoke to someone," he said, "but I couldn't see. It may have been Emma, her cook."

"I don't think so. A woman would be wearing light-colored clothes in this weather. I only had a sort of glimpse out of the corner of my eye, but I got the idea that it was a man, fairly tall."

"But—" said Jeremy, and then was silent. He was puzzled. He had learned already that Clive's eyesight and hearing were very much more acute than his own, but he had no idea who the man could be.

"It makes no odds," said Clive. "Nobody's going to stop us now. All that matters is that Mickey and I should get into the house. Sal, too, if she can manage it." He looked at the luminous dial of his watch. "She'll have just left the cave. I'll give her a call to let her know we're on our way."

"Will she answer?"

"No. She won't have her trumpet. She'll be working round the center, and she doesn't want to draw attention to herself. If some of them come chasing up here, so much the better. We'll have to move fast as soon as I've played it."

They were in a little glade. Clive unhitched his trumpet and paused for a moment, warming the mouthpiece. Then he played a call Jeremy had not heard before, a longer one, gay and lively and defiant. The silvery notes streamed up like a challenge into the still air. They were drowned before the finish by Prince's deep, excited barking and by the barking and howling of other dogs in the distance, and the startled movement of animals, a general stirring and commotion that seemed to spread out around them like the ripples on the water when a stone is dropped into a pool.

But by then the boys were off and away, springing down the glade like will-o'-the-wisps, like mocking spirits haunting the dark woods of Castlecombe.

CHAPTER 8

the "wanderer's song"

THEY TOOK LONGER THAN THEY HAD IN-tended to reach the Stooping Lady. Prince's wounds were troubling him. He was limping badly and his tongue was hanging out. He needed a drink, and so they went a longer way round, making for a spot where a stream splashed into a small pool on its way to the river. For that matter, they were not sorry to have a drink them-selves.

They were on lower ground here. The woods were thinner, broken by paths and glades and open spaces, so that torches could not be used. It did not trouble Clive, who had an almost uncanny gift for picking his way through the darkness. A glance at the deep purple sky, the outline of a tree or a rock, was all he needed to give him his bearings.

This part of the woods was filled with life. There was movement everywhere. Bodies crashed away from them through the bushes. A herd of deer went stampeding off down a glade, having probably caught Prince's scent. A flock of sheep scattered in all directions as they crossed an open space. A dog came running up to them, barking furiously, to go off howling after Clive had let fly with his catapult. And more than once they had to take cover as they heard the sound of hoofs drumming along the bridle paths. The keepers were evidently out in force that night.

But things went well for them, and nothing untoward occurred until Clive suddenly stopped and stood intently listening.

"They're hunting again!" he said.

The baying of bloodhounds sounded in the distance, faint but ominous, like an ugly answer to the challenge of the trumpet call. A little shiver ran down Jeremy's back. They stayed stock-still while they listened, and Jeremy found it hard to determine the direction from which the sound was coming, but finally Clive gave a soft chuckle.

"I think I know what they're doing. They're taking the hounds up onto the ridge, to the place where the boar was killed. They know at least one of us has been there, and they're hoping to give them a fresh scent. They'll be able to do it, too, if I'm the one they're after. But they're going to have a jolly long run for their money! They're moving away from the center while I'm moving in, and I bet I can go faster in the dark. Come on!"

They sprinted now, and did not pause until they had reached the copse of elm trees directly behind the Stooping

Lady. Clive then hooted three times, like an owl, and they waited, but there was no reply.

"Sal isn't there yet," he said. "She probably nipped up a tree and waited when she heard the hounds. She'll be along. You must go by yourself now, Jeremy. I don't want to lay a scent running right up to the tor. Follow this path, and when you get out in the open you'll see it straight ahead of you. It's quite an easy climb, but go gently—go on your hands and knees, don't use your torch. You can't miss the hollow. Remember, you and Sal are to stay there, and not budge for anything, until you see the rocket. If it doesn't work I'll sound a trumpet call. All right?"

"All right," said Jeremy, keeping his voice steady. "Good luck, Clive."

Clive put a hand on his shoulder.

"We'll do it," he said, seeming at that moment much older than his fifteen years. "We'll manage. Don't be afraid. And then Castlecombe will be ours again—and yours, too, Jeremy. You'll be our friend always. Remember that!"

He gave him a little shake, called softly to Prince, and vanished into the darkness with scarcely a sound.

The darkness seemed to deepen with his going, and Jeremy was assailed by a terrible loneliness. The Park seemed to become a different place, huge and hostile, filled with lurking presences, eyes that peered and ears that listened, men and beasts on the prowl. Jeremy stayed quite still for some moments, then he braced himself and began hurriedly to grope his way along the path, feeling that he must move at once or he would become too terrified to move at all.

The path was small and overgrown—a badger track, probably. It seemed a long time before he reached the edge of the copse, but once he had done so he felt better. There was light. Fifteen yards ahead of him the huge black bulk of the tor rose up against a clear, star-scattered sky. He sprinted across the strip of rough grass and began to climb.

There were moss and small shrubs to help him at first, but then nothing but smooth bare rock. It was steeper than he had expected, not a difficult climb by daylight for a boy wearing sneakers, but tricky at night. He went cautiously on both hands and knees as Clive had advised, up the Lady's back and over her shoulders, until he reached the hollow. It was a pool of darkness, like a saucer three or four yards across with a jagged rim of rock. He slipped down into it and found it still warm with the heat of the day's sunshine. And this was wonderfully comforting. In the center of the darkness Jeremy felt suddenly safe, as though he had reached a place where nothing could touch him. He had been on the move for an hour and a half, covering a distance of four or five miles. Sally had given him some barley sugar, and he fished a piece out of his pocket and began to unwrap it. For the first time since he had left the cave he was able to rest.

For a while he did not think of anything, or pay any

attention to the stir of life that was going on around him. But gradually, as his breathing grew quieter and the beating of his heart subsided, he began to distinguish between the sounds that came to him out of the night, some distant and some close at hand.

He heard the movement of animals over the grass of the King's Vista, on the other side of the tor; the occasional bleat of some small creature for its mother, and the mother's reply; the drowsy twitter of birds that were not yet asleep, the singing of crickets, the whir and hum of night-flying insects, and a faint, insistent mutter which, although he did not recognize it, was the croaking of bull-frogs down by the river.

All these were homey and peaceful sounds, but there were others. He heard the barking of dogs now and then, the drumming of hoofs, and once or twice the voices of men. The keepers were being very active about something, and perhaps this was because Mungo McDougal had given them special orders. The baying of bloodhounds still reached his ears occasionally, but far distant. It seemed that Clive must be right, and that they had taken the hounds to the place where the boar was killed, on the other side of the ridge. And then perhaps they would follow the path by which Clive and he had come, round and down by the stream, then round again and within fifty yards of the tor. But they were bound to move slowly in the dark, and Clive would be a long way off by then. Jeremy felt sure that he would be safe in his hollow—and Sally, too, if she had got there in time.

But time was passing, and Sally had not yet arrived. Jeremy thought of her in the darkness, a twelve-year-old girl armed with a stick and a catapult, with dogs and animals and keepers to contend with. So many things could happen! He dared not let himself think about them. He told himself that it would be all right. Sally would come because she was Sally, because she was a Palfrey. She was sure to come.

And presently he perceived that the world was changing. It was growing lighter. He stood up and looked over the rim of the hollow. A brilliant three-quarter moon, more gold than silver, was rising like a lordly ship through the tops of the trees on the ridge.

The light grew rapidly, and after a time Jeremy dropped back again into the shadow of the rim, feeling that his hiding place was no longer as safe as it had been. But he got over this, and since Sally still did not come he was overtaken by a restless itch to explore. Climbing was easier now. Taking care not to show himself against the skyline, he scrambled out of the hollow and up over the Lady's head, until he was lying on his stomach looking down at the King's Vista.

He saw a widespread scene of moonlight flooding over a grassy expanse broken here and there by a big, isolated tree; a scene of light and shadow, of velvet and silver, so soft, so hushed, that it seemed not so much a sweep of grass lit by moonlight as a true valley on the moon.

The tor stood about halfway down the broad, stately avenue, making a break in one of the two rows of chestnuts that flanked it. Over to his right Jeremy caught a gleam of water from the Bird Lake, and to his left, about half a mile away, was the house.

It stood on higher ground than the tor, surrounded by trees and hedges, and seeming at that distance nothing but a dark mass, with only the fortress tower and the chapel belfry clearly distinguishable in the moonlight. Jeremy gazed at it in fascination, imagining the huge cluster of roofs and chimneys hidden by the trees. He caught gleams of light, but could not tell whether they came from uncurtained windows or from the lanterns of people moving about outside. He heard the barking of dogs.

And presently he turned his attention to the scene immediately below him. The avenue, more than a hundred yards wide, was dotted with the forms of animals, some moving about but the greater number lying in separate groups on the grass. There seemed to be hundreds of them, cattle and sheep for the most part, of strange foreign breeds that would be worth examining if one could see them more clearly. These were the animals whose peace the fireworks were intended to disturb.

A small herd of antelope came trotting up the avenue after drinking, heads alert, ready to take flight under the trees at the least alarm; a strangely humped cow moved slowly across, followed by her calf. Beyond the chestnuts on the far side there were yet other things to be seen, as Jeremy knew from the map Sally had drawn. There was a grove of lime trees in which was a little ruined walled garden—paved walks and statues and a fishpond—which some early Palfrey had made; and not far from it there was an apiary with twenty beehives. Jeremy gazed about him in wonder, so entranced by the tranquil beauty of the scene that for a little while he forgot all other things. But suddenly he was brought back to earth. He saw a figure on horseback, a keeper, riding quietly down the far side of the avenue.

He thought instantly of Sally. How long had he been lying there? She might have slipped into the hollow and be waiting, wondering what had happened to him. He began to wriggle backward, keeping low as before, but moving rather hastily. Getting down was more awkward than he had expected. There was a steep part at the back of the Lady's head. He slithered the last few feet and landed with a bump in the hollow, accompanied by a little shower of stones.

The hollow was still empty.

Jeremy had just time to realize this, and to wonder in anguish what had become of Sally, when something happened which caused him to drop into the darkest corner of the hollow and stay huddled there, holding his breath. He heard the tread of a leather-soled shoe on the smooth rock below, and a man's voice called softly but sharply:

"Who's there?"

Jeremy stayed still as the rock itself.

"There's someone there," the voice said. "If you're one of McDougal's people I'd better warn you that I'm armed with a Webley revolver. Don't do anything foolish. But if you're a Palfrey you've nothing to fear."

The voice was a pleasant one, not at all like that of a keeper. But Jeremy did not move. It could easily be a trap.

"I shan't come to look for you. It might be awkward for both of us. And I can't tell you my name till I know who you are. But I'm a friend of the Palfreys. I can assure you of that."

Jeremy was tempted. It was the sort of voice one trusts. But McDougal had arrived that day, perhaps bringing other people with him—a detective, for instance. It could so easily be a trap.

"A difficult situation," the voice said with a light laugh. "We can neither of us be sure, can we? I'll tell you what I'll do. I'll recite a little poem. If you're a keeper, I must apologize—you'll be bored, I'm afraid. But if you're a Palfrey you'll understand."

And he recited:

"How fine, how white the roads run
To the mountains dim;
How brave, how blue the seas roll
To the world's rim!

"See how they beckon, the distant lands
That sing strange songs, that raise strange hands
To lead me on, though I go unshod
Where never the feet of men have trod. . . .
And these are the high rewards I crave:
The white sail swaying across the wave,
The quest, the promise, the urgent breeze,
The far, faint peaks and the secret trees;

The tower, the temple, the city wall—
Oh, I must seek and know them all,
And reap this wealth 'neath the boundless sky
Till, rich with life, I turn home to die!

"How keen, how clear the stars shine
In God's great room;
How softly shall my bones rest
In Castlecombe!"

There was a little pause.

"Well?" the voice said.

And Jeremy moved at last. He was certain now. He got to his feet, saying with a little gasp:

"You can come up if you like. There's no keeper here. I'm not a Palfrey, but I'm a friend."

He looked over the rim and saw the man a few yards below him, standing out in the open on the smooth slope of the Lady's back. He was wearing clothes that looked dark in the moonlight, a tweed jacket and slacks, perhaps; and he had a hat pulled down over his eyes. The moon was at his back. He seemed not to be worried by the risk of being seen, but his manner was very alert. He glanced swiftly up at Jeremy, then looked away from him, so that he might have appeared to be just standing there, not talking to anyone.

"Keep your head down," he said. "The bloodhounds seem to be coming this way."

Jeremy had grown so accustomed to the distant noise of the hounds that he had half forgotten them; but now he realized that they were very much less distant. There was a sudden loud burst of baying, as though they were crossing an open space.

"Come up quickly!" he said. "They won't come here. They may go through the copse."

"No, I won't come up. Too risky for you. You're Jeremy Shepherd, aren't you? I read your message. I want to tell you something quickly. This thing you're doing—is it a plan to get into the house?"

Jeremy hesitated in utter astonishment and then said: "Yes."

"Well, go on with it, and don't worry about me. Tell Clive and Sally. I'll get back here if I can, but don't wait. Now get well under cover and stay put. There may be some shooting in a minute."

"What are you going to do?" asked Jeremy.

"Something about those bloodhounds, for a start. I shan't hurt anyone."

The man gave another laugh, then turned and ran down the slope and across the grass, to vanish under the trees of the copse. His voice, his laugh, his movements were all like Clive's; but this did not surprise Jeremy, who knew already that he was a Palfrey. What had taken his breath away was the realization that this was the man whom Clive had caught a glimpse of when they shot the arrow to Aunt Eleanor.

Jeremy got down under cover again, his heart beating furiously and the thoughts tumbling through his mind. The hounds were drawing nearer, but not very fast. Clive had said that they would have to be on leashes in the dark, with men running on foot; and there were countless scents to divert them. Several minutes went by. The baying grew louder still, and Jeremy thought they must now be approaching the copse. Suddenly there was a pistol shot.

The sharp report was followed by instant commotion, the voices of men shouting, cursing, and questioning, and then the blast of police whistles. There was no indication that anyone had been hurt, but the hunt seemed to have been thrown into utter confusion. After a minute there was another shot.

And this was followed by a fusillade as the keepers used their shotguns. A minute passed, sounding like a battle. Then there were voices again.

"This way! Get after him! Bring the dogs along—don't worry about anything else! This way, I tell you! Come on! Come on!"

There were more shots after an interval, as the keepers reloaded their guns and fired wildly into the dark. But they were farther off. The voices were growing fainter. The hunt was being drawn away from the tor and back toward the ridge.

Jeremy found that he had had his clenched fist pressed to his mouth, and that his body was stiff and numb as though he had been lying in the cold. The world was growing quiet again, and the danger seemed to be over. But he was alone once more, and as he remembered Sally he began to be afraid.

What had happened to her? What would he do if she did not come? He knew what he had to do. It would be useless to try to look for her. The plan must go on, whatever happened. When the signal was given, he would have to carry out their part of it by himself, and then find a hiding place for the night. The thought made him very miserable, for Sally's sake far more than for his own. What could have happened to her?

And suddenly a shadow, silent as a ghost, appeared over the rim of the hollow. Sally's voice spoke to him, and he could not restrain his cry of delight.

CHAPTER 9

the stampede

SALLY HAD PUT ON A DARK BLUE JERSEY and black stockings pulled over her knees, so that nothing of her was visible in the darkness except her hands and face. She sat panting and gripping Jeremy's hand, too breathless for speech, and Jeremy fished a piece of barley sugar out of his pocket and gave it to her.

"Golly!" she said at last, with a shake of her hair. "Things do seem to be happening tonight! I'm jolly glad I've got here. There were keepers everywhere, it seemed like dozens, that's why I took so long. But who on earth started the shooting? It can't have been Clive."

"It was a man," Jeremy said. "He—"

"He shot low over their heads. I saw the flashes. He wasn't trying to hit anyone. But the keepers were! They'd have got him if they could!"

"How far away from them was he?"

"Oh, a fairly safe distance. He wasn't taking too many

risks. But he was obviously trying to draw the hunt after him, as though he were on our side."

"So he is," said Jeremy. "He's a Palfrey, you see."

Sally stared at him open-mouthed, and he told her exactly what had happened. For a few moments she was silent, and then she asked:

"What was the poem about?"

"About the call of distant lands," Jeremy said slowly. "The roads and the sea, and mountain peaks, and towers and temples, and—"

" 'And reap this wealth 'neath the boundless sky, till, rich with life, I turn home to die.' Jeremy, was that it?"

"Yes, that was it."

"The 'Wanderer's Song'!" Sally sat with her hands covering her cheeks, gazing at nothing, as though a great wonder had taken place. "Oh!" she said softly. "Oh, Jeremy."

"I expect you know who it is now."

"I can't be certain. There are so many it might be—cousins or uncles. If one of them should have guessed that we're here, and if they thought it worth while to help us find the Casket and the Sword. . . . But there are other family songs they might have thought of. They need only have quoted three or four lines and we'd have known it was a Palfrey. But that particular song . . . And he said he'd try to get back here?"

"Yes, but he said to go on with the plan and not wait for him. I still wasn't sure if I ought to tell him that the idea was to break into the house, but I did. He didn't say what he was going to do, but of course he'll try to help."

"He's doing it already. Listen!"

The stir in the Park had been growing while they talked in low voices. They had heard several more shots from the depths of the woods. And now there were sounds of movement coming from the direction of the house—horses and the shrilling of whistles.

"It sounds as though more keepers were going after him. So much the better for Clive and Mickey. He's doing our job for us! Oh, Jeremy, this is wonderful! I was feeling a bit miserable just now—all these beastly keepers, and so few of us! But now everything's changed. I'll tell you one thing. We won't think any more about going back to the cave. We must certainly get into the house!"

"Yes!" said Jeremy, his heart leaping. "Oh, yes!"

"We shall have to do some thinking. Do you remember the map?"

"Pretty well. Anyway, I climbed up on top and had a look round. It's going to be a job to get across the Vista, with this moon."

"I know. It'll be just a matter of sprinting when we get the chance. But the thing is, we may easily get separated. We've got to have a meeting place on the other side." Sally thought for a moment. "The apiary's best. You can use the Lady to get your bearings. It's almost dead opposite, about twenty yards beyond the chestnuts. You can't miss it, Jeremy. There's a fence round it to prevent animals knocking the hives over, and there's a shed at the end nearest the house. Whoever gets there first will just lie and wait in the long grass by the shed. It'll be perfectly safe."

"All right," said Jeremy, a little dubiously. "Provided the bees don't come and sting us!"

Sally laughed.

"Bees stay in their hives at night, they don't go gadding about like us! We ought to start sorting out the bangers and fuses. It must be nearly time for the rocket to go up."

Sally had brought a supply of fireworks in a paper bag stuffed under her jersey and kept in place with a belt, but Jeremy's store was larger. They had fixed small stones to some of the big bangers, using adhesive tape from a first-aid outfit. The idea was to make them heavier, so that they could be lighted and flung a considerable distance, like hand grenades. They stuffed their pockets and saw that they both had matches and lengths of slow-burning fuse; and while they were doing this they heard the sound of horses in the avenue. A man's voice called:

"Everything all right?"

The voice that answered was evidently that of the keeper who had been watching over the animals. They had not heard him, but he must at that moment have been quite close to the tor.

"It's quiet enough here. What was all the shooting about?"

"One of the kids seems to have got hold of a pistol. Shooting at the hounds, I suppose. He might have killed someone. They're trying to get him."

"First it's those blooming trumpets, then it's catapults, and now it's pistols! I'm getting fed up with this job, Sam. I reckon it's time the boss called in the police."

"Don't be a fool! What d'you think the local coppers could do? Are you scared of a pack of kids? The boss is offering fifty pounds for the first one that's caught. Then we'll get to their hide-out, and then we'll round up the lot."

"Fifty pounds!" There was a low whistle. "Sounds as though the boss was scared of 'em, even if you aren't! How many of 'em d'you reckon there are?"

"I don't know. It looks like they may have brought in some of the village kids to help. I'd say a dozen, at least. They seem to be all over the Park."

At this point Sally had a silent fit of giggling. A dozen of them! It showed what you could do by sounding trumpet calls in the dark! She sat there quivering, while Jeremy gripped her arm, terrified that she would explode. And suddenly one of the men exclaimed:

"Hey, look at that!"

They had both seen it at the same instant, and Sally's giggles stopped abruptly. A rocket had gone streaming up from amid the trees on the southern ridge, to burst, high over the Park, in a cluster of red and green and golden stars.

Jeremy struck a match and crouched over it, cupping the flame in his hands. They lighted two six-inch lengths of the fuse—which Mickey had made of tow treated with saltpeter and a little paraffin—enough to go on smoldering for a quarter of an hour. They could hear the keepers still excitedly talking while they tried to make up their minds what to do. And a thought came to Jeremy. He whispered quickly in Sally's ear, and before she could say anything he had scrambled out of the hollow and up onto the Lady's head.

He worked his way forward until he was looking down onto the avenue. The keepers were still there, three of them, seated on their horses in a little group not more than twenty yards away. They were still excitedly talking and staring in the direction from which the rocket had appeared. Glancing round, Jeremy saw a bright red light high up amid the trees of the ridge. It was the first of Mickey's flares. He heard one of the men say:

"Cripes! They're setting the woods on fire!"

Jeremy had a large firecracker in his hand. He touched it with the smoldering end of his length of fuse and flung it at the nearest horse. Then, without pausing, he lighted another, one of those with a stone attached, and flung it as far as he could in the other direction, toward a group of cattle lying on the grass.

He could not resist waiting an instant to see the result. The keepers had heard nothing. They were still staring toward the ridge, where another flare had just broken out. One of them was saying, "I'd better get back to the house and—" At this moment the first cracker went off, with a report like that of a cannon, under the tail of the horse Jeremy had aimed at.

He saw it rear high in the air, and waited to see no more. He wriggled backward, scrambled down into the hollow, which was now empty, and sprinted over the Lady's back and across the grass to the copse, hearing the second cracker explode as he ran.

Sally was waiting for him at the edge of the copse. They ran together without saying a word, passing through the copse and then working their way round until finally they came to rest in the long grass at the foot of one of the big chestnuts fringing the avenue, about a hundred yards from the tor.

They had heard sounds of great commotion as they ran, the shouting of startled men, the shrill note of a police whistle, the lowing of calves and cattle and the drumming of hoofs. They saw a great, packed herd of cattle moving at a trot down the avenue toward the lake, while all around them were the sounds of other animals, the less sluggish ones, breaking away under the trees.

"Oh, Jeremy, that was grand!" breathed Sally. "Now we've got to keep them moving. We ought to try and work them round along the river. The country's more open this side of the avenue. What's happened to the keepers? I can't see—"

At this moment they saw a riderless horse.

It must be the one that had reared up when the firecracker exploded. Having thrown its rider, it had bolted and perhaps been headed off by one of the other men. It had slowed down now, and was cantering diagonally across the avenue in their direction. It was coming quite

close to them, its speed dropping to a trot as it approached a bunch of cattle moving slowly ahead of it.

Jeremy heard Sally exclaim, "Oh—oh!—" and then she darted from his side.

He watched her run after the horse. She clutched the reins and then the saddle, heaved herself across its back, and swung her leg over. Then she pulled the horse's head round and came back to where he was still standing under the tree.

"I'm going to drive them from the other side. You let loose your bangers on this side—keep under cover!—and then nip across when you get the chance. Be careful, Jeremy. The apiary, don't forget!"

She kicked the horse into a gallop and rode out toward the center of the avenue, lying forward with her head against its neck. Jeremy heard her shouting at the top of her voice, "Git up, you lazy cows! Git up!"

Then he lost sight of her. He was on his own again.

He could never afterward say much about that wild quarter of an hour during which Sally and he, working independently from opposite sides of the avenue, drove the animals down toward the lake and along the open ground by the river, drawing half the keepers after them and leaving the way clear for Clive and Mickey to break in on the far side of the house. It was all too confused, a breathless succession of incidents in moonlight and in shadow, rough and dangerous and sometimes terrifying, but so thrilling, so wonderful and strange, that you could never tell it properly; you could only make a song about it.

He ran out into the avenue and threw two more fireworks in quick succession, not caring where they went—the noise was all that mattered. The cattle were well on the move again. He returned to the shelter of the chestnuts and sprinted toward the lake, keeping close to the trees not only as a precaution against keepers but also to save himself from being trampled underfoot. Even so, he had some narrow escapes.

He felt wonderfully alive, and it seemed to him that he had grown much older. All that day he had been learning things, gaining in alertness and experience, picking up the Palfreys' trick of seeing and listening all ways at once. He darted in and out from under the trees, lighting and flinging his fireworks, working his way down the avenue and hearing the reports of Sally's fireworks from the far side. It was not long before he heard keepers as well

A party of at least half a dozen came galloping down the center of the avenue, spreading out as they came. He heard shouts and the blowing of whistles, and then the crack of their stock whips as they rode in among the cattle, trying to check their wild stampede and prevent them plunging into the lake. Sally, far ahead of them and at the edge of the lake itself, was doing the same, lighting and flinging fireworks to divert them along the open land by the river.

Jeremy had to be more careful now. He could not leave the shadow of the trees. But he went on flinging fireworks as long as he dared, until a sudden shout from a keeper warned him that he had better stop. He was very near the bottom of the avenue by then, within fifty yards or so of the lake and the river, and the screeching and cackling of the waterfowl on the lake were new sounds added to the tumult of the night. He turned and plunged into the thickets, darted across a clearing, and climbed the first tree that came handy, not resting until he had reached the safety of its upper branches, where he clung like a sailor to the mast of a ship in a storm.

Whether the keeper had spotted him or not, he did not seem to have come after him. Jeremy took the chance to get his breath. He could see the cattle moving along by the river in a dense mass, the great herd of rare and valuable beasts collected from all over the world; and presently he made out the forms of keepers trying to get ahead of them and slow them up. He heard the lowing and the bellowing, the shouting voices and the cracking whips; but he heard no more fireworks, and saw no sign of Sally. He hoped she had slipped off her horse on the far side of the avenue, and was now making her way under the lime trees to meet him at the apiary. He had used up most of his fireworks. This part of the battle was over, and it was time for him, too, to be making for the meeting place.

He could see the tor clearly from his treetop, only about a quarter of a mile away, and he decided that the best thing was to go back there and then cut straight across. He climbed down and started toward it, leaving the sounds of tumult behind him as he ran. He was tired without knowing it, and he ran slowly, encountering no keepers but having to dodge animals that had strayed under the trees. Finally, when he was near to the tor, he turned again toward the row of chestnuts and stood under one of them, looking over the moonlit grass. He had a little shock. The avenue was empty, swept clean. Gazing to right and to left, he saw not a living creature, man or beast.

He would have liked to rest for a minute or two, but he dared not waste this chance. The moon was as bright as ever, the avenue huge and bare except for a tree with spreading branches almost directly ahead of him, standing by itself like an island in a London street. Someone might appear at any moment. He decided to sprint for the tree and pause in its shadow before going the rest of the way.

He drew a deep breath and started, bending low and keeping his head down; and when he felt the shadow of the tree close over him he slowed up with a gasp of relief.

It was only then that he saw a man seated on the ground with his back against the trunk. A hand reached out and grasped him by the ankle before he could draw back. A voice exclaimed:

"Got you, my lad!"

CHAPTER 10

in the great hall

JEREMY WAS YANKED OFF HIS FEET AND pressed backward onto the grass with two powerful hands gripping his arms. The man knelt over him, giving a low chuckle.

"Better not try to struggle, matey! You'll only get hurt. And if you yell I'll give you a clout you won't forget. Are there any of your pals about?"

Jeremy did not answer. He made an attempt to wriggle free, but the grip on his arms tightened savagely and he had to give it up. The man was much too strong for him. He lay motionless and silent, staring at the dark face poised above him in the shadow and seeing the gleam of white teeth.

"Not going to say anything, eh? Well, it won't do you any good, even if there are."

The keeper leaned with his forearm across Jeremy's chest while he released one hand to pull a police whistle out of his breast pocket. He blew three long blasts, glancing about him as he did so, as though he half-expected to see an army of Jeremy's friends advancing to the rescue. But the moonlit grass was empty. Distant sounds of commotion were still coming from the direction of the river, but they seemed to be dying down.

"Let's 'ave a look at you," the keeper muttered. "Kids swarming all over the blessed Park, and you're the first I've clapped eyes on!"

He pulled Jeremy to a sitting position, and they confronted one another. Jeremy had his lips pressed tightly together, partly because he was determined not to say anything but also to stop them trembling. The suddenness and shock of his capture had brought him very near to tears. He was trying miserably to think what the result would be. The most important part of the plan would probably not be affected. With any luck, Clive and Mickey would have broken into the house by now. But what of Sally, who might at that moment be waiting for him in the apiary? What would she do when he did not come?

"About twelve, aren't you?" the keeper said. "Cor! What d'you think you're playin' at? Are you one of the village boys? Well, all right, you don't have to tell me if you don't want to. The boss'll have it out of you soon enough. What's in this bag of yours?"

His manner until then had been rough but good-humored, as though he were too pleased at having made a capture to be really angry. But suddenly it changed. His hands were exploring the contents of the shopping bag, which Jeremy now wished he had had the sense to empty. He brought out a firework and peered at it for a moment, uttering a low growl in his throat. Then he gripped Jeremy by the shoulder and shook and cuffed him, half-shouting as he did so:

"So it was you, was it? You're the one that had me off my horse? It shook me so bad I can't hardly walk! I'll be bruised for a week, if no worse! I might have broke my perishin' neck!"

Jeremy bore it in silence, keeping his mouth tight shut and gazing steadily at the man while his face grew white. The keeper stopped abruptly, as though he had suddenly remembered that he had only a twelve-year-old boy to deal with. He was not a brutal man, simply a very angry one; and not without reason, after all.

He went on in a quieter voice:

"There was another of us brought off his horse this morning—with a catapult, or something. And now it's fireworks—and guns, too! Are you kids trying to kill someone? What d'you think you're playin' at?"

"I'm sorry you were hurt," said Jeremy with a little gulp. "I didn't mean you to be. I wanted to start the horses galloping, that's all."

"Start the horses galloping? By gum, you did it, all right! But what's the idea, anyway? What's it all for?"

"We want to drive you out of Castlecombe. You don't belong here," Jeremy said.

"Meaning you do belong here—eh?"

Jeremy did not answer this. The keeper was silent for a moment, as though he were thinking it over.

"I'm not saying we belong here. I wouldn't want to, come to that. This moldering old place, it fair gives me the creeps—and you kids playin' your trumpets out in the dark! . . . But then, who does belong here? Who belongs in a place like this in these days? You tell me!"

This time Jeremy had no need to answer. They heard the sound of a horse cantering toward them over the grass.

The keeper jumped up, seeming to have forgotten his bruises. He pulled Jeremy to his feet and dragged him out into the moonlight, still keeping a tight grip on his arm.

"Hey!" he called. "Look what I got!"

The mounted keeper uttered a low whistle as he reined his horse alongside them.

"So you've caught one! How did you manage it, Jim? I thought you couldn't walk?"

"Never you mind how I managed," said the man Jim. "I done it, that's what matters, and I'm the one that gets the fifty-pound reward. I reckon I deserve it, too. He's the one that had me off, Sam. He don't deny it, and he's still got fireworks on him, an' that's proof."

"All right," said Sam. "The boss'll deal with him. I'll take him to the house."

"Have they caught my horse?"

"Not yet. It's down there somewhere. It looked like one of the other kids was riding it for a time—it can't have been this one."

"They haven't caught him, too?" asked Jim sharply, evidently worried about his fifty pounds.

"No. They've had their hands full with the cattle. Some

of 'em went into the river. A fine mess those kids started! Here, lift the boy up and I'll take him in front."

Jeremy drew a deep breath. His heart had leaped at the news that Sally had not been caught. She must now be at the apiary, perhaps within earshot. He yelled at the top of his voice:

"Sally, they've got me! Don't try—"

It was all he had the chance to say. A heavy hand was clapped over his mouth with so much force that he felt as though all his teeth had been loosened. Jim growled:

"I told you I'd knock your block off if you yelled!"

"So that means there may be others near," said Sam coolly. "Sally, eh? That'd be the Palfrey girl. Let him yell if he likes, and if they come after him maybe we'll catch a few more. You'd better stay under that tree for a bit, Jim, and keep your eyes open. Let Frank and Benny know if they come by. There's not much use trying to look for these kids till we know where their hide-out is. We've just got to wait."

Jeremy was lifted into the air, struggling fruitlessly. He was dumped astride the horse's shoulders, and Sam's arm went round him.

"So long, Jim."

"Don't forget," said Jim. "I'm the one that gets the reward."

The horse broke into a trot. It was an uncomfortable ride for Jeremy. Sam's arm was tightly round him. He seemed to be some kind of leader among the keepers. He spoke with a voice of authority, cool and matter of fact.

"Don't try to wriggle clear, son. It wouldn't do you any good, even if you managed. We're out in the open, and I've got a whip that I know how to use. I'd whip the feet from under you, and you wouldn't like that."

Jeremy at that moment was too miserable and dispirited to try. He was still a little dazed by the blow Jim had given him. His lips were swelling, and he could taste blood in his mouth.

The moon was high in the sky. They seemed to Jeremy to go a long way. As they reached the top of the avenue the house loomed up ahead of them, standing on higher ground, surrounded by a wide girdle of grassland, its gardens protected by a high hedge lining a wooden fence. They followed this hedge until they came to a gateway from which a carriage drive ran across the grass to another of the avenues, the one leading to the main gates of the Park, about a mile and a half distant. All this was strange to Jeremy, but he was not paying much attention in any case. A man opened the gate for them, but there were trees, so that it was too dark to see what he was like. He and Sam exchanged a few words, and then they followed the drive round the house, past shadowy lawns and terraced gardens, until they came to the huge outer courtyard with buildings on three sides.

A dog barked at their approach, and others joined in, so that the night was filled with the barking of dogs. Sam blew two blasts on his whistle. He rode up to a broad flight of steps leading to a porch with stone pillars, and here he dismounted, lifting Jeremy down to the ground.

An electric lantern sprang to light under the porch. There was the creak of a bolt and the rattling of a chain. One wing of the lofty door opened, and there appeared a short, very fat man in shirt sleeves, smoking a pipe. He was collarless, his waistcoat was unbuttoned, and he was wearing carpet slippers. Jeremy guessed instantly that he was the caretaker, Moggs.

They were still standing at the foot of the steps, Sam with one hand gripping Jeremy while with the other he held his horse.

"Hey!" he said. "Isn't there supposed to be someone on duty out here?"

"There is," said Moggs in a wheezy voice. "To say nothin' of two or three more patrolling round the house, and others inside. And where are they all? Chasin' about the Park, skylarkin' after a pack o' kids. There's no one here but me and the missus. The dogs was barkin' something frightful a little while ago. I went round to the back to have a look, but I couldn't see nothin'. Anyway, it ain't my business—"

"All right, all right," growled Sam. "Where's the boss?"

"He's in the house somewhere, far as I know. I 'aven't seen him for an hour or more. He isn't in the library or in 'is bedroom, I know that. He could be anywhere. I don't know what he's doing. You could search the place an hour on end and never—"

"Stow it, can't you! You talk too much. Can't you see what I've got?"

"Course I can," said Moggs, who had indeed been staring hard at Jeremy all the time he was talking. "About time, too! Why don't you bring 'im up so I can see 'im proper?"

Sam tossed the reins over the stone ball surmounting one of the stone pillars at the foot of the steps, and escorted Jeremy up to the porch. Here Moggs inspected him still more closely, peering at him with small piggy eyes in a big sallow face.

"And who might you be?" he demanded. "I never set eyes on you before. You're no connection of the family, I'll take my oath, and you don't look like one o' the village boys neither."

"Jim Willis caught him," said Sam. "He was chucking fireworks about, and he got Jim thrown off his horse. He's still got some fireworks on him."

"What's your name?" asked Moggs, scowling at Jeremy. "Come on, let's have it! Don't you try any funny business with me, my lad!"

Jeremy yawned in his face. It was not a make-believe yawn. The crowded events of the day and the night had been too much for him. He was suddenly so overwhelmed with tiredness that he could no longer think or care what happened, or even be afraid. He stood there swaying slightly, scarcely able to stay on his feet.

"The kid's half-asleep," said Sam. "Take him inside."

"I'll find a way to wake 'im up," said Moggs with a wheezing chuckle.

They passed through a doorway, across a lobby, and

through another set of doors into a hall at which Jeremy glanced without taking in many details. It was big and lofty and somber, being lighted only by a crystal chandelier hanging by a chain from the ceiling. A wide stairway ran up one side to what seemed to be an overhead gallery. The place felt chilly, despite the warmth of the night. Round a huge, empty fireplace were grouped chairs and a table and a couch on which a little sharp-faced woman was seated knitting. She jumped up at the sight of Jeremy.

"So you've got one at last!" she exclaimed in a high-pitched, grating voice. "But who is he? I don't recognize him."

"Seems 'e don't want to tell us," said Moggs with the same gasping chuckle. "I'll soon find out!"

"No, you don't," said Sam calmly. "That's the boss's business, not yours. You go and fetch him."

"I told you, didn't I?" said Moggs. "He went off by himself without saying where. There's over two hundred rooms in this house, and 'e could be in any of 'em."

"Well, go and look for him. I'll keep an eye on the kid. The boss said he wanted to be told the minute we caught one."

Moggs scowled, his little eyes screwed up.

"Why should I do the chasing about? If you're so keen on finding 'im—"

"You know the house and I don't," said Sam. "Now go on, before I get cross."

He had not raised his voice, but it was clear that Moggs

was a little afraid of him. Glowering and muttering, he picked up a bunch of keys and an electric farm lantern from the table, and shuffled down the hall in his carpet slippers to vanish through an archway.

Jeremy meanwhile had sat down on a straight-backed chair and was gripping the arms to hold himself upright. His lips were hot and sore; he was scratched and bruised and very thirsty. He mumbled:

"Could I have something to drink?"

"Well, listen to that!" exclaimed Mrs. Moggs. "He comes trespassing on other people's property, and not so much as a 'beg your pardon'! All he does is ask for a drink!"

"It won't hurt you to fetch him a glass of water," said Sam. "Come to that, I'm thirsty myself. Bring a few bottles of beer, missus, and some glasses. Some of the others'll be coming back soon, I dare say. What's the time?"

"Getting on for midnight, as you'd see for yourself if you looked at the clock."

Mrs. Moggs and Sam stared at one another in silence for a few moments, and then she got to her feet.

"Well, I suppose I've got to fetch the drinks, seeing as it's for *you,* Mister Sam Cosset! If you ask me, there's too many people giving orders in this house!"

She departed in her turn, going out by a doorway under the stairs.

Sam turned to Jeremy. He put a hand on his shoulder and shook him, but not roughly.

"Wake up, son. You needn't be scared of me. I want

to talk to you. I want you to tell me something. What's the lay?"

He bent down to look closely at Jeremy, who gazed drowsily back at him. He was a powerfully built man with a broad tanned face; but it was not a brutal face, and his eyes were not unfriendly. When you saw the keepers at a distance in their dark shirts, with their whips and guns, they seemed strange and inhuman; but after all they were not very different from other men.

"The boss don't tell us anything," Sam went on. "We're paid to do our job and keep our mouths shut, not to ask questions. Supposedly we're here to look after the animals, but a fat lot he cares whether the animals are looked after or not! Our real job is to guard the place—stop anyone getting in, and catch 'em if they try. It's not so easy, in a place this size! And what's the reason for it? There's only one, that I can see. There's something here that the Palfreys want. And the boss wants it too—if only he knew where it was!"

Jeremy's wits were coming to life again. He had followed most of this. He asked after a little pause:

"Is—is McDougal searching for something?"

"So you know his name, do you? Mungo McDougal, that's him! Well, if he isn't searching for something, what is he doing? Why has he gone ferreting about the house at this moment, instead of being somewhere where we can get at him, with all this bother going on in the Park? There could be anything hidden in this place—gold, jewels, money, anything. You tell me what it is, son, and maybe I could help you get it. I'm not so sold on McDougal. I'm not a crook, neither. I wouldn't ask more than a fair reward."

"McDougal won't find it," Jeremy said slowly. "And you couldn't either, and neither can I. Only a Palfrey can find it."

"Meaning, they know where it is, but they won't tell?"

Jeremy shook his head.

"It isn't like that. It's—it's different. I can't explain. It's to do with the family, you see, and—it's all so old."

Sam wrinkled his forehead.

"My oath," he muttered, "the place is old enough, I'll grant you that! But all the same . . . You've got to think of yourself, son. You're in trouble. You may want a bit of looking after. McDougal can be a rough customer if he chooses, and he's not the sort to let anything come between him and what he wants. And there's your pals to consider. What chance do you think you've got, a parcel of kids, against a man like that?"

Jeremy did not answer. While he listened other things were stirring in his mind—the voices of Clive and Sally, the notes of a trumpet in the darkness, the words of songs.

"Even if you don't know where the stuff's hidden, you must know something," Sam urged. "I'd sooner be a friend than an enemy. I don't like fighting against kids. You tell me, and I'll help you if I can."

"It's no good," said Jeremy, and smiled faintly. "Even if I wanted to, I couldn't tell you anything that would be any use. I've never been in this house before. But it isn't what you think. It isn't just us against McDougal. It's McDougal against Castlecombe. That's what it really is."

Sam continued to stare at him with a puzzled frown. Then he turned abruptly away as Mrs. Moggs came back into the hall.

CHAPTER 11

mcdougal and the bat

JEREMY DRANK A GLASS OF WATER AND felt better. Sam seemed to have lost interest in him. Jeremy went and curled up in a more comfortable chair, and fell into a sort of doze without quite losing consciousness of the two people watching over him—Sam sitting by the table, drinking beer and smoking cigarettes, and Mrs. Moggs seated upright on the couch, clicking her needles and now and then giving a sharp, disapproving sniff.

They spoke to one another occasionally. Mrs. Moggs started to complain in a high, querulous voice, talking about "goings on" and the police. Sam said:

"Why don't you get off to bed? You've no call to be sitting up."

"I'll wait for my husband to come back, if it's all the same to you, Mr. Cosset," said Mrs. Moggs with another sniff.

"He's taking a deuce of a time," said Sam.

Jeremy heard this without paying much attention to it.

The words seemed to come from a distance, like the thoughts and questions that were crowding through his mind, as though one part of his brain were asleep and another part still awake. Had Clive and Mickey got into the house? Where was Sally? What were they going to do to him?

Although his eyes were closed it seemed to him that he could still see the immense, lofty hall, dimly lighted by its crystal chandelier. There were big framed pictures on the walls of men and women who must be long-dead members of the Palfrey family, the ancient lords and ladies of Castlecombe. There were also old weapons on the walls, a suit of armor in one corner, a tall grandfather clock whose tick could be heard like the slow beating of the house's heart. Jeremy did not remember having looked at any of these things, but he knew they were there.

"The dogs are barking," said Sam suddenly. "Round at the back, by the sound of it."

"That's not the first time," said Mrs. Moggs. "We heard them before, Moggs and me, but—"

"I ought to go and have a look," said Sam. "But I can't leave you alone with the kid. You'd never catch him if he took it into his head to slip away, and he'd be gone in a flash. Why the dickens doesn't Moggs bring the boss back?"

"No doubt he's still looking for him, like you said, Mr. Cosset."

"Unless he's sneaked away to have a drink on the quiet," Sam muttered. "Or perhaps he thought he'd go searching for something on his own—like other people in this house!"

The voices seemed to fade away. The hall was quiet and still, but not really peaceful. It seemed to Jeremy to be wide awake, just as a part of his own mind was wide awake—as though the portraits on the walls were watching and waiting for something to happen.

But he must have fallen really asleep in the end, because he was suddenly startled by the sound of loud voices, most of them strange to him. He half opened his eyes. A number of the keepers were standing round the table, talking, drinking, and filling the air with tobacco smoke. One was Jim, the man who had caught Jeremy.

They were taking no notice of him, and he shut his eyes quickly. The sleep had done him good, although it could not have lasted long. He was stiff and sore, but he felt alive and alert again.

". . . Chased him pretty well to the top of the ridge an' then lost 'im," one of the men was saying. "The hounds wasn't no manner of good. It must 'ave been one of the others, because they hadn't got his scent."

"It's this playin' with guns that I don't like. What kind of gun d'you reckon that was?"

"Dunno. He didn't know how to handle it anyway, didn't allow for the kick. The shots went way over our heads."

"Perhaps he wasn't tryin' to hit anyone."

"The one that got Bob with a catapult this morning—he was trying, all right!"

"Come to that," said Sam's voice, "your shooting doesn't seem to have been so good, either."

"Go on! He knew enough to keep out of range. Anyway, a bit of a peppering with small-gauge shot wouldn't 'ave done 'im much harm. Serve 'im right!"

"That's what I say! What do they think they're up to, these blinking kids? Bolting the cattle with fireworks! There's a steer with a broken leg, and I'll bet you we'll find there was more than one drowned in the river. What are they doing it for?"

"Well, we've got one of 'em now, so per'aps we'll find out."

There was a pause, and Jeremy guessed that they had turned to look at him. He kept his eyes tightly closed.

"Still sound asleep!" one of the men muttered. "Bloomin' little nipper—looks no more than eleven year old!"

"I'm the one that caught 'im," said the man Jim, "and I get the reward. Don't nobody forget that!"

"You aren't giving us much chance to forget it, are you, mate? But fancy offering fifty pound for a little perisher that size! There's something behind all this, and I reckon it's about time the boss told us what it is."

"Why not ask him?" said Sam with a faint laugh. "He wouldn't want to have any secrets from you!"

"All right, you can make a joke of it if you like, Sam Cosset, but I say we're entitled to know. It didn't matter when all they did was run about the Park playin' their trumpets—a sort of a kids' lark, as you might say—but—"

"Those trumpets make me fair hoppin' mad! I hate the sound of 'em! Just havin' a game with us, that's what it is."

"They broke into the house, too, don't forget."

"Well, but it doesn't seem they took anything except the trumpets. Why didn't they just come and ask for them, if that's all they wanted? If it's the Palfrey kids, I don't see why the boss should 'ave refused."

"The boss wasn't here then. You know what the orders were."

"Of course I know. But what does it all mean? It isn't just trumpets now, or even bows and arrows and catapults—it's guns and fireworks. Next thing we know, they'll be trying to set the house on fire. You can't talk about a kids' lark any more. There's something behind it, and what I say is, why's it being kept secret from us? I reckon it's time we went to the boss and said—"

The speaker broke off abruptly. There was a sudden dead silence and then a new voice spoke from somewhere above their heads. "Well, Dan Trumble, and what would you say?"

It was very different from the voices of the rough, commonplace men who had been speaking. It was the voice of a boss, a man of power, not overloud, but harsh and arrogant and sure of itself. Even before he opened his eyes Jeremy guessed that Mungo McDougal was descending the stairs.

Peeping cautiously, he saw him, a man in tweeds coming deliberately toward the group of silent men round the table. His thick hair was turning white, which made him look old; but he stood as upright as a man of any age. He was over six feet in height, burly, bulky, and solid, standing squarely on his feet, with broad, powerful shoulders, a bullet head, a thick neck, and a heavy-jawed, tight-lipped face.

He paused at the foot of the stairs, as though waiting for what Dan Trumble had to say; but the keeper's courage seemed to have failed him. He muttered something and then was silent. Nor did anyone else speak for some moments. The men were suddenly as subdued as a classroom of schoolboys when the headmaster unexpectedly walks in.

The boss glanced toward Jeremy, who quickly closed his eyes, with a vague idea that it would be better for him to go on pretending to be asleep. Sam said:

"We got one of the kids, sir."

"So I see," said Mungo McDougal. "Why wasn't I told?"

"I sent Moggs to tell you. Didn't he find you, sir? He said he didn't know where to look."

"That's true. He didn't know. Where I've been is no business of his, or of yours either. I haven't seen him."

"Then where's he got to?" asked the voice of Mrs. Moggs. "Why hasn't he come back?"

"I don't know, missus, and I don't care. He'll turn up, I dare say. Meanwhile I want to hear about this boy. Where did you catch him?"

Sam started to tell the story. Jim chipped in to say that

he was the one who had caught Jeremy, and that a reward had been promised—but McDougal cut him short, telling him roughly that he'd get his money if he didn't talk too much. After this no one interrupted while Sam described the happenings in the Park. When he had finished McDougal said:

"One of them used a firearm? You're sure of that?"

"Certain," said another of the men. "It could have been a service revolver by the sound of it."

"But no one was hurt?"

"No, sir. We don't know if he was really trying to hit anyone."

"You don't know that he wasn't! Well, it all looks pretty bad. Trespassing, using firearms and catapults, stampeding the animals with fireworks. . . . You say this boy was caught with fireworks on him?"

"There's some in the bag he was carrying, sir. I've got it here."

"Good. We shall have plenty to tell the police, if I decide to call them in."

"Yes, sir. We was just thinking, after what's been happening tonight—"

"Nobody asked you to do any thinking. I'll decide. I certainly didn't intend to bother the police with this nonsense. It seemed to me a poor look-out if a party of over a dozen grown men couldn't deal with a handful of children. But I agree that what has happened tonight has changed the situation. They're obviously getting help from outside. Well, I shall have a talk with this boy in private. If he tells me what I want to know, we'll be able to settle the business without any fuss. If he doesn't, it'll be very much the worse for him and for all of them. That's all."

There was a brief pause followed by a stir of movement. Jeremy kept his eyes tightly closed, but now his blood was running cold. He was terrified by this talk of the police.

"The dogs were barking a little while ago," McDougal said.

"Yes, sir," said Sam. "There was only me here at the time, and I couldn't leave the boy. We—"

"Why the deuce didn't you send some of these men out directly they came back? Why are they hanging about here? Three of you get off at once. Work round the house and examine all ground-floor windows to see if they've been tampered with. Two more of you had better do the same from the inside. You'll have to try and find that fool Moggs, because he's got the keys. Where are the rest of the men?"

"Still trying to sort out the animals, sir."

"Well, when they come back they can go on guard in different parts of the house. Keep two of them here in case of emergencies. And stay here yourself, Cosset. If anything happens, anything in the least suspicious, I want to know about it at once. I shall be in the library with the boy."

"Very good, sir."

"There's one other thing. Listen, all of you. You're

being very well paid for your work, and you know it. There's no stinting. If you're kept up all night you'll get extra, and in any case there'll be a fat bonus for everyone at the end of this month. But that's provided you carry out my orders. You'll keep your mouths shut about everything that goes on in this place, and you won't go poking your noses into my business. Is that understood?"

There was a murmur from the men.

"All right. Now get going."

For a minute or two the hall echoed with the sound of voices and footsteps as the men were detailed for the different jobs. Then it grew quiet again. Jeremy had not moved or opened his eyes, but now he was made to do so with a start. Mungo McDougal said:

"Get up, boy. I know you're shamming."

Jeremy got to his feet, feeling foolish and frightened at the same time. McDougal was standing over him. He gripped him by the hair and thrust back his head, gazing intently at him.

"Are you a relation of the Palfrey family?"

"No," said Jeremy.

"H'm," said McDougal, still studying him. "Well, whoever you are, you're going to tell me. We'll go along to the library. Now march!"

He seized Jeremy by the collar of his shirt and thrust him toward the stairs.

When they reached the top of the stairs Jeremy saw that what he had thought was a landing was in reality a very big room containing settees and armchairs, tall glass-fronted china cabinets, pictures, and a grand piano. He had only time for a quick look at it. They passed under an archway into another room, even larger, with a splendid painted ceiling, but with its furniture shrouded in dust covers.

"You needn't be scared," McDougal said, his voice less harsh now that he was out of earshot of his men. "You'll be all right if you have the sense to know what's good for you. But don't try any tricks. I'm a bad man to play games with." He seemed to want to make Jeremy feel that he bore him no ill-will. He went on in a confidential tone: "Reception rooms, these are, for state occasions. They've had kings and queens visiting this house. Ever seen one like it before?"

"No," said Jeremy.

"Ah. And likely you never will again. There's not many left of the great houses where the dukes and lords used to live. They're done for, lad. They've gone out like the bows and arrows your friends, the Palfreys, are so keen on."

Jeremy said nothing. They passed through another room as big as the last, but also shrouded in dust covers. McDougal had been switching lights on and off, glancing keenly about him. But after switching off the lights at the end of this room he produced an electric torch.

"You know something?" he said. "Less than a fifth of this house has electric light—only the central part and one or two lines to special places, such as the library. The old man put in a lighting plant about thirty years ago, but nowhere near big enough. Couldn't afford to do the job properly! So everywhere else it's oil lamps and candles, like in the Middle Ages."

There was an oil lamp burning over the short stairway they descended, but the corridor beyond it was in darkness.

"I'll tell you another thing," said McDougal. "There's about fifty bedrooms and only five bathrooms. Five, that's all! And one telephone! You'd think there'd be a dozen, at least, in a place this size; but no, only one, stowed away in a cubbyhole off the Great Hall, so you have to have someone on duty there all the time if you want to know when anyone rings up. That's the Palfreys for you! Never any money to spare for keeping the place up-to-date. And you know why? Because the old man chucked it all away building that wall!"

They turned along a dark passage running off at right angles, and after they had gone a little farther McDougal stopped. He got a key out of his pocket and gave it to Jeremy.

"Open that door, lad."

Not until they were inside the library did he relax his grip on Jeremy's shirt. He switched on lights and locked the door behind them. They were in a fair-sized room entirely lined with books and containing no furniture except a central table and a stepladder for reaching the higher shelves. But beyond a communicating archway was a bigger room with tall book cupboards, tables and armchairs, standard lamps, two busts on pedestals, a chessboard, and a radio-phonograph; a modern room, in short, except for the huge hooded fireplace. McDougal pointed to another communicating arch.

"That's the study, next door, where the old man used to write his letters and see after his affairs—if he ever took the trouble! And then there's yet another room, and they're both of 'em full of books. They say there's about twenty thousand books altogether—twenty thousand! I'd like to know whoever read all that many books! Sit down there, lad, by the fireplace."

Jeremy did as he was told, sitting on the edge of a big armchair. There was a pile of logs in the fireplace but no fire. McDougal took a big cigar out of a box on the table, and after lighting it stood gazing down at him with the smoke eddying about his gray bullet head. He startled Jeremy by smiling suddenly.

"You must have had fun tonight, slinging those fireworks about!"

Jeremy could not withhold a small answering smile, and McDougal chuckled.

"I know! I've got up to a few larks myself in my time. I wouldn't want to be hard on a pack of kids. And I don't bear malice toward those that try to fight me. I've been fighting all my life. But I win, son—I always win!"

His expression changed abruptly. The smile vanished. His face and his voice grew hard.

"Have you thought what'll happen if I turn you over to the police? There'll be bad trouble all round. The police won't see anything funny in the things you've been doing tonight. The law's been broken a dozen times over, and you know it. They'll ferret everything out, trust them for that! There'll be trouble for the young Palfreys and for everyone that's helped them. And plenty of trouble for you, my lad. You were caught with fireworks on you, don't forget. You've got parents, I suppose? What do you think they're going to say?"

Once again his expression changed, becoming more amiable.

"But if you tell me what I want to know, I promise I'll see you get safely home in the morning, and not a word said. What's more, there might be a present. What's your bicycle like? I might know where to put my hands on a new one, with every gadget you ever dreamed of. What do you say to that? So now you be a sensible lad and answer a few questions. To start with, what's your name?"

Jeremy had had time to think. Although the thought of the police still terrified him, it made him angry as well. He had a feeling, which he could not have explained, that McDougal was cheating in some way. He was cheating, and perhaps he was also bluffing; and the offer of a new bicycle only seemed to make it worse. In any case, Jeremy had made up his mind what he was going to say.

"My name's Jeremy Shepherd and I live in London," he said slowly. "I had measles, and so a few days ago I came to stay with my aunt, Miss Eleanor Shepherd, who lives in a cottage quite close to here. I heard Clive and Sally Palfrey playing trumpet calls in the Park, and that's how I got to know them. They asked me if I'd like to come in,

and I said I would. I've been here since this morning, and I helped them with the fireworks, and that's all I'm going to tell you."

There was a little pause. McDougal blew a cloud of smoke.

"That's all, is it?" he said gently.

"Yes."

"You aren't going to tell me where the young Palfreys hide and sleep at nights?"

"No."

"Or who's helping them—fetching in supplies and suchlike?"

"No."

"Or what it is they're looking for?"

Jeremy shook his head vigorously. McDougal smiled, seeming not at all put out.

"All right, lad. I'll answer the last question myself. They're looking for the Casket and the Sword."

His smile broadened as he saw Jeremy start slightly.

"You didn't expect me to know that, eh?"

"I suppose Moggs could have told you," Jeremy said defiantly. "He might have heard the story. He's been here a long time. But it doesn't make any difference. You needn't think you're going to find them. Only a Palfrey can do that."

"But no Palfrey has," said McDougal. "They've been hidden in this house for hundreds of years, so the story goes, but no Palfrey has found them. And it wasn't Moggs that told me. I wouldn't set much store by anything that old fool might say. Shall I tell you how I know? It's because I was born here. That's the truth of it, lad—I was born in Castlecombe."

Jeremy gazed at him, speechless with astonishment, and McDougal chuckled.

"That's taken your breath away! It might surprise Master Clive and Miss Sally, too, not that they'd think anything special of something that happened in the servants' quarters, nigh on sixty years ago. That's where I was born. There were forty-odd servants in the house in those days, and my mother was one of them. A housemaid she was, and my father was a groom."

He stood chuckling at Jeremy's amazement.

"Aye," he went on, "and here I grew up to be a stable lad. There was no going to the pictures in those days—no motorcycles—nothing to take you away from your work. Here I was and here I stayed till I was sixteen, and scarcely ever went outside the Park. Work from morning till night, and precious little pay. It was fine for the rich folk in those days; they could treat their servants how they liked! But I wasn't going to be anyone's servant. I had ambitions, d'you see? I reckoned I was as good as they were, and maybe a bit better. So I ran away."

For an instant anger blazed in McDougal's eyes, as though the recollection of those days when he was a stable-boy in a rich house still rankled, after so many years. But then he smiled again.

"I went off to make something of myself, and, by gum, I've done it! I traveled over half the world, seeking my fortune. It was a rough battle I fought, plenty of ups and downs, and more downs than ups at the beginning. But in the end I won, like I always do. I began to get rich; and while I was going up the Palfreys were going down.

I was watching them! I hadn't forgotten. Sooner or later I meant to come back to Castlecombe!"

Thoughts and discoveries were coming to Jeremy as he listened, like lights suddenly dawning in his mind. He thought of the "Wanderer's Song." This might have been a tale told by one of the Palfreys, a tale of roving and seeking; but it seemed that it was not only the Palfreys who were drawn back to Castlecombe! He thought of something else as well. He recalled the words of old Jeremy Palfrey's prophecy—". . . a stranger, yet not strange."

"But not as a servant," McDougal went on. "My oath, no! Not as a poor man. I meant to come back as a man rich enough to own the place—and meaning to have it! I knew when the earl was in trouble over money; but he didn't know me! I'd changed my name long before that. He didn't know who it was when he found there was a Mr. Mungo McDougal in the City who was ready to lend him all the money he wanted. He didn't know it was the lad who had groomed his horse when he was a young man, and walked it round the paddock to cool off after he came back from his ride. He'd give me a tip now and then, five or ten bob it might be, and throw me a civil word the way you throw a dog a bone. Did he think I was grateful? I hated him! I hated all of 'em—the gentry! What made them any better than me? Sixteen years I was here, roaming the Park whenever I got the chance to slip away—aye, and having a peep inside the house, too, although I wasn't supposed to go near the parts where the fine folk lived. Do you think Master Clive Palfrey knows this place any better than I?"

At this moment a queer thing happened. There was a slight sound from the chimney; some soot fell and a bat flew into the room, causing Jeremy to start back on his chair. McDougal stood watching it for a moment as it circled blindly in the light. Then he picked up a folded newspaper from the table and went after it, moving with astonishing nimbleness for so bulky a man, and struck it down in mid-air. He dropped the senseless body onto the open hearth and set his heel on it, chuckling as he did so.

"Still pretty spry, eh, at my age! But that's Castlecombe for you, lad. Moldering and decay everywhere. Bats! . . . Well, you saw how easy I knocked it down. That's how I'll treat the Palfreys, if they get in my way!"

He was wiping his fingers on his handkerchief.

"I've been away on a business trip to Canada. I didn't get back till the night before last. If I'd been here, do you think young Clive would have been allowed to make fools of my keepers the way he has? Trumpet calls and catapults and fireworks—it's enough to make you laugh! Not that I hold it against him, mind. I can respect anyone that puts up a fight. But what chance do you think those children have against a man like me?"

He stood over Jeremy, holding the fat cigar between the fingers of his powerful hand.

"And what makes you think they'll find the Casket and the Sword before I do, after all the time the Palfreys have had to look for them? I know what the prophecy says, but I'd sooner trust common sense than prophecies. I've had surveyors on the job, measuring and hammering and writing down all the places where there might be a secret room or cupboard—any sort of hiding place. There's hundreds of nooks and crannies, I'll grant you that; but who d'you think's likely to get there first, the Palfreys or me? . . . And yet, d'you know something? I don't want their Casket and Sword. I wouldn't waste time looking for them, if it wasn't to stop the Palfreys getting them. I don't care about the money, I've got plenty. At the end of this month the loan expires, and then Castlecombe will belong to me. After that the Palfreys will be welcome to come and search for their Casket. I don't care if it's brimming with diamonds. There's only one thing that matters to me, and that's Castlecombe!"

He seemed to grow larger as he spoke, and Jeremy lay back in the armchair, wretched and despondent, crushed by the sheer strength of the man. He asked with a little quaver in his voice:

"But why do you want it so much? What good will it be to you?"

"It's where I was born," said McDougal. "I want it to be *mine!*"

He turned away and began to walk up and down the room, jingling the coins in his pocket.

"But not the way it is now. My oath, no! First thing I'll do is to pull down this old rabbit warren of a house and put a new one in its place—steel and concrete, five stories high, or ten if I feel like it! A new house for the new world—*my* house! And I'll lay out gardens such as you never dreamed of, with every flower and bird and beast in the world, and floodlight them at night! I'll have an airfield and a hangar for a dozen planes. And I'll have the great ones of the earth to come and visit me—not just the lords and ladies, although they'll come fast enough, I'll warrant, if I ask 'em—but the real bosses, the people who own and build and run things—the men like me! That's what I'll do! And then—"

He stopped abruptly. For the moment he had forgotten Jeremy, but as he remembered him the glow died out of his face and his voice changed.

"But that's enough. You don't want to sit here any longer, listening to me talk. It's time for you to do the talking, lad. We'll make it short and sweet, and then you can go to bed. There's only one thing I need to know. Where's the Palfrey children's hide-out? Where do they sleep at nights?"

Jeremy did not answer, but he began to sit slowly upright.

"It seems certain they don't go outside the Park," McDougal went on. "They must have rigged up a shelter somewhere in the woods, a tent or suchlike. You'd think those fools of keepers would have found it by now. Once I know where it is I can put my hands on them and settle this business without any more fuss. I won't hurt them, I promise you that. So just you tell me, lad."

There was a pause while he waited. But now Jeremy was smiling and no longer crushed. Suddenly everything was changed.

"You don't know as much as you think you do," he said.

McDougal stared at him, thunderstruck.

"What's that? What d'you mean?"

Jeremy was trembling a little, but he went on in a clear voice:

"If you knew the Park as well as Clive and Sally you wouldn't have to ask me about the hide-out. You'd have guessed the most likely place and sent someone to look. But it isn't only that. You don't really know Castlecombe at all. You may have been born here, but you're a stranger just the same. There are so many things that you don't understand. You think the trumpet calls are silly, but they aren't. And you don't understand about songs."

"Songs?" McDougal repeated blankly. "Are you raving, boy? What are you talking about?"

"They're jolly important," Jeremy said. "It's no use asking me to explain. All I know is that you don't belong here, and Clive and Sally do. I don't think you're going to win, either. The Palfreys aren't done for. They're cleverer than you think. And I don't care what you do, I'm not going to tell you anything more."

McDougal took a pace toward him, his face suddenly vicious; and Jeremy cowered back, thinking that he was going to be hit or manhandled. Indeed, something of the kind might well have happened had there not been an interruption. Suddenly there was a knock at the door.

McDougal stopped and turned, looking toward the outer room.

"Who's there?"

"It's Moggs, sir. It's urgent, if you don't mind."

"All right," McDougal said. He looked quickly at Jeremy. "Stay where you are, boy. Don't try any tricks, or it'll be the worse for you."

He went to the door and unlocked it.

"Well, what is it? Have they caught the Palfreys? Come in, man—don't just stand there!"

Moggs's voice was clearer now. He sounded strangely nervous.

"If you wouldn't mind stepping into the passage, sir. It's something you might not want the boy to hear."

"Very well."

McDougal went out, closing the door behind him.

A sound from the chimney caused Jeremy to jerk round. There was a little scuffle, a shower of soot, and Clive dropped into the hearth.

His face was black but his eyes were bright. He grinned and beckoned.

"Come and join the bats!" he said.

CHAPTER 12

the flickering light

THERE WERE FOOTHOLDS IN THE WALL OF the chimney, and then iron rungs like flattened croquet hoops, dating from the days when small boys were sent up to sweep chimneys by hand. Jeremy remembered *The Water Babies*, and how Tom, the sweep, had lost his way in the maze of chimneys in a big house, and had come out into the wrong room, to find himself staring at a beautiful little girl in bed. The room into which he and Clive emerged was also a bedroom, but there was no one in it.

"Try to clean up a bit," whispered Clive, wiping his feet on the hearthrug. "We don't want to leave a trail of soot."

"How on earth—?" said Jeremy.

"We captured Moggsie and used him as bait. Mickey must have been just beside him when he knocked at the door, sticking him up with a gun. It was only a wrench, really." Clive was listening intently while he whispered.

"The thing is, are they going to chase Mickey or are they coming after us?"

A cavernous sound came up the chimney, the booming echo of McDougal's voice. The words were not distinguishable, but it was not hard to guess the sort of things he was saying. Clive gave a little snort of amusement.

"He came back to look for you. Well, he won't try to climb the chimney, that's certain! We'll go."

He led the way across the room and they ran on tiptoe, plunging into an older part of the house where the rooms were smaller, the ceilings low, the passages narrow, winding and uneven, with steps at unexpected places.

They encountered no one, although they heard sounds coming from below. But presently they saw a pale glow of light ahead. Clive went forward cautiously and then beckoned to Jeremy. The light came from an oil lamp on the lower landing of a stairway. There were men not far away from it, they could hear their voices; but Clive led the way up a narrow flight of wooden stairs that grew darker as they ascended. The stairs creaked, and they had to take great care. At the top was a door which Clive unlocked with one of Mickey's master keys, locking it again after they had passed through.

"It's us!" Clive called softly. "I've rescued the prisoner." He flicked a torch about. "Watch how you go," he said to Jeremy. "We've made a zareba at the far end."

They were in a long, low attic which looked as though it contained the dust and lumber of a hundred years. They picked their way through. The "zareba" was a small, cleared space fenced in by a strange assortment of objects—a marble-topped washstand on which stood an old dolls' house, a chest of drawers, a battered rocking horse, a tin hip bath, some dingy oil paintings in tarnished frames, and two packing cases. And in the middle of it was Sally.

She and Jeremy hugged one another in rapture.

"Did you hear me yell?" Jeremy asked.

"Yes, rather! It was awfully brave of you. But I saw them take you off, in any case. I was lurking under the chestnuts, looking out to see if you were coming. So then I just had to follow Clive into the house. It was easier than I'd expected, although the dogs were troublesome. And then—"

"Pipe down!" said Clive. "Don't talk so loud."

He had pried two short lengths of board out of the floor, leaving a rectangular hole large enough for a person to get through. But Jeremy was puzzled as he looked at it. The light of the torch showed a flat wooden surface only a few inches below the level of the floor.

"We're just over our playroom," Sally whispered. "That's the top of the big toy cupboard. We made it into a secret exit ages ago. We only did it for fun, but it may come in useful now."

Jeremy grinned. His heart was singing. He was back in a world that was quite different from McDougal's world, and he found it hard to believe that he had thought, even for a moment, that McDougal might win.

"So that's something else about Castlecombe that McDougal doesn't know!" he said.

"Pipe down, for the love of everything!" said Clive.

He was crouched over the hole, listening intently. But after a moment he came and sat beside them on the dusty floor, switching off his torch and leaving them in pitch darkness.

"All right so far. But Moggsie will have told them that the house is swarming with invaders, so they're pretty sure to come snooping round here. We shall have to wait for a bit. Do you know something, Sal? McDougal was born in Castlecombe."

"What!" Sally exclaimed.

"So that explains a lot of things. He sort of half believes in the Casket and the Sword. Poor old Mungo! He isn't such a bad old crook, really. He's mad keen to own the place. He wants to put up a whacking great modern house with an airfield. I must say an airfield isn't a bad idea."

From the whispered conversation Jeremy could piece together what had happened. Clive and Mickey had had very little difficulty in breaking into the house, since the numerous diversions in the Park had largely stripped it of its guards. They had started on the business of picking locks and opening doors, and while they were doing this Moggs had come shuffling along in his carpet slippers calling, "Mr. McDougal, sir, where are you?" They had waylaid him and forced him to go with them down to the cellars, and there they had proceeded to frighten the wits out of him.

"Mickey told him all about the Chinese tortures he'd studied when he was a lad," Clive said with a chuckle.

"They sounded jolly gruesome! But the fact is, Moggsie was so scared since he heard someone had been using a real gun in the Park that he was ready to believe anything."

He had told them of Jeremy's capture, and Clive's first thought had been for Sally, guessing that she would now try to break into the house. He had gone to meet her, leaving Mickey in charge of Moggs. Then, after installing her in the attic, he had gone along to the Great Hall to investigate. He had been lying at the edge of the room overlooking the hall, hidden under a settee, when McDougal had appeared; and when he heard that Jeremy was going to be taken to the library he had at once thought of the way to rescue him, knowing what he did about the chimney. But it was necessary for McDougal to be out of the way for a minute or two, and that was where Moggs came in. Clive had hurried back to the cellar to arrange things with Mickey, who was to wait a little while, to give him time to get into the chimney, and then escort Moggs to the library, keeping the handle of a monkey wrench thrust into his back as though it were a six-shooter. Once Moggs had knocked on the library door Mickey was to withdraw along the dark passage, pretending still to keep him covered. It was risky, with the keepers starting to patrol; but the house was so enormous that the chances had been good.

"It's still risky," Jeremy said. "Moggs must have told McDougal as soon as he thought he was safe. There are probably more keepers back in the house by now. It won't be so easy for Mickey to get away."

"I expect he'll manage," said Clive. "He's done a good many odd jobs in the house at one time and another. He knows his way about."

"Will he go back to the cave?"

"Not just yet. There's another thing he's going to try to do first. We think it may give them rather a surprise, if it comes off." Clive chuckled softly, without explaining. "We may be hearing from Mickey before long."

And while Moggs was being taken to the library, Clive had climbed into the chimney from the room above. He had overheard most of the conversation between McDougal and Jeremy. At one moment he had sent down a shower of soot, and it was a lucky thing that McDougal had thought it was caused by a bat.

"Come to that, he might have heard me before if he hadn't been so busy talking," Clive said. "I think he's one of those people who can't resist talking about themselves. He went on and on, Sal, all about how ghastly it was being a stable lad, and how he hated the gentry, particularly Grandfather. Can you imagine anyone hating Grandfather? All he really wanted was to know where we've been hiding, so that he could round us up. He doesn't know about the cave, of course. But Jeremy didn't tell him. Jeremy was terrific. He made a jolly fine speech at the end, and told him where he got off."

Jeremy felt himself blushing in the darkness.

"I suddenly felt sure he was bluffing," he said.

"About the police?" said Clive. "I wonder. We've broken the law in about twelve different places, there's no getting away from that. Just the same, he obviously isn't a bit keen on bringing the coppers in. Well, anyway, we shall be calling all the bluffs if things work out."

Jeremy did not quite understand this. But there were still so many questions. What had become of the other Palfrey, the stranger who had recited the "Wanderer's Song"? Clive and Sally did not know. Nothing more had been seen or heard of him. But they seemed quite untroubled by this. It was enough that he was there and knew what was going on.

And what of the Casket and the Sword, the mystery of the hiding place? They did not answer this question either. Sally said:

"We shall find them. Don't you worry."

Clive said:

"You'll see. It will all work out."

Their voices were light and gay and yet had a note of gravity, as though they were filled with a strange wonder. They were so sure of themselves! But McDougal had been no less sure.

Jeremy thought of the huge difference between them. Anyone could understand McDougal's reasons for being sure. He was rich and powerful; he was in occupation of the house, with a small army of men to carry out his orders. Those were good, solid reasons. But the Palfreys' reasons were of quite another kind. They were sure because they were the Palfreys, because they belonged, because they were very old and still young. Their reasons were of a kind that vanished and seemed absurd when you tried to explain them—old dreams and memories, and trumpet calls and songs.

Jeremy thought these things, or half thought them, not clearly understanding, while they sat close together in the darkness. There was a sort of lull in the battle. They were waiting until it was time for the next move. And suddenly Clive stirred. He flicked on his torch for an instant, then went and crouched over the hole in the floor with his head bent, listening.

His ears were so sharp! A full half-minute went by before Jeremy heard a muffled sound of movement and voices coming from below.

Clive very carefully put the floorboards back in place, and then came and whispered to them.

"They may come in here. We'll hide in separate corners. If they spot one of us, the other two must bolt."

A few minutes later they heard footsteps on the wodden stairs. The door was rattled, and then a key turned in the lock. The light of an electric lantern shone dimly at the far end of the long, low place, and Moggs's wheezy voice said:

"Well, you can ferret round in here if you want to, but there's about a mile of attics in this house, and no more reason why they should be in one than another. If we're going to try to search behind everything and under everything we'll be at it till doomsday. And I still say they're more likely to be in the cellars, which is where I was took."

The man with him muttered something and came farther into the attic. He seemed to come about halfway, moving gingerly amid the lumber. Then there was a crash and a thud, followed by a flow of strong language. He had evidently stumbled over something, and perhaps (Jeremy profoundly hoped so, as he lay huddled under an old bedstead, holding his breath!)—perhaps he had hit his head against a beam.

"Blast everything!" he muttered. "The door was locked, anyway. There's no sign of anyone in here. Come on, let's go down."

They went out again, relocking the door behind them.

The torch flickered, and the three of them drew together again. Clive was quivering with laughter.

"You'd think he'd have half stunned himself, but I suppose you can't hurt solid ivory! I was terrified in case they had the sense to look for our footprints in the dust!"

He had put back the floorboards in order to conceal the hole. Now he took them out again, and they all crouched over the hole, listening. After a minute or so they heard men enter the playroom, immediately below. Every sound was audible. Moggs and the other man had evidently been joined by a third, and they tramped round the room inspecting every corner of it and muttering to one another as they did so.

"This door wasn't locked," one of them said.

"The lock's been broke for years," said Moggs. "The

young varmints did it themselves—on purpose, most likely."

There was a creak within a foot of the motionless listeners as the door of the toy cupboard was opened.

"The stuff they collected! Ever see so much junk?"

"Well, they're not in 'ere, anyway. We'd better be getting on. We've got the bedrooms to do."

The men went off and could be heard more distantly, moving in and out of the adjoining rooms. But at length these sounds died away, and after they had waited a little longer Clive said:

"I'll go down and see if the coast's clear. Sal, shine your torch."

Jeremy now saw that two rusty screws projected from the top of the toy cupboard. Grasping these, Clive lifted out a roughly cut section, across the ends of which thin projecting strips had been tacked to hold it in place. The hole in the cupboard was only a little smaller than the hole in the floor.

"Back in a minute," Clive said.

He slipped down through the hole, muttering "Darn!" as his foot touched something in the cupboard that rattled. Then the cupboard door creaked again, and then there was silence. They did not hear him cross the room.

He was away for what seemed a long time, while Jeremy and Sally waited breathlessly, keeping close together. The silence of the house was filled with muffled sounds. It was a huge relief when at last they heard his voice whispering below them.

"All clear! But we must be careful. They're on the floor below, and there's a man by the stairs. Jeremy, you first. Lower yourself down and I'll guide your legs. The cupboard's full of stuff."

Jeremy did as he was told and a moment later was standing unsteadily with one foot on the floor of the cupboard and the other on a box of some kind. Clive helped him out into the room. Sally followed, and then the door of the cupboard was carefully closed.

They were in a low-ceilinged room with two small windows through which a milky light filtered, making it seem almost bright after the pitch darkness of the attic. Jeremy wondered if it could still be moonlight. How long was it since Mrs. Moggs had said that the time was getting on for midnight? How many hours had passed? He had no idea.

He peered at the toy cupboard, which was so tall that its top came within an inch of the ceiling, quite hiding the hole. There were other cupboards in the room, a window nook, a big battered table littered with objects, a butterfly cabinet, fishing rods, two wicker armchairs, a bookcase, a cottage piano, and a fireplace with a guard. Jeremy was gazing about him in the dim light, half seeing and half guessing, fascinated by this room which was Clive and Sally's own. But then he noticed that they had drawn away from him and were standing by themselves with their heads almost touching, holding each other by the hand. He whispered:

"Are you going now for the Casket and the Sword?"

"Yes," said Clive.

A pang went through Jeremy's heart.

"But—but you won't want me."

Sally turned at once and reached out a hand to him.

"We do, Jeremy! We do!"

Clive took his other hand.

"You've talked yourself into it," he said with his soft laugh. "It was that speech to McDougal! You're part of us now."

Jeremy was filled with a radiant happiness. He stood tightly gripping their hands.

"But do you know—?"

"We must go the way we went before," said Clive. "That's all."

"Go the way we *feel,*" said Sally, "like in a dream. Something will happen. You'll see."

"It started in the passage, outside the bedrooms," said Clive.

Like in a dream! Jeremy felt that he was living in a dream. They went out into the passage, which was darker than the room, although there were one or two small windows in the opposite wall giving onto an inner courtyard. They moved to their left until they were standing at the door of Sally's bedroom. Beyond it was Clive's room, and beyond this was the stairway, where a faint light shone from below. They could hear movement and a murmur of men's voices, but the Palfreys paid no attention. They were standing motionless, one on either side of Jeremy.

"He came that way," said Sally, pointing toward the far end of the passage, which was lost in darkness.

"Yes. Then he turned and we followed. That's the way we go, Sal, and round to the Tower House. It was the Tower House, I'm sure."

"Yes, the Tower House, and then—"

But the words were whipped out of Sally's mouth by a sudden tremendous sound—the tolling of a bell.

It was the bell in the chapel belfry, the Great Bell of Castlecombe. To the Palfreys and all the people of Castlecombe, and to the dwellers in the countryside for miles around, it was the voice of great and solemn occasions, rejoicing and sorrow, birth and death, peace and war; a voice of the past, speaking for the present and calling to the future, the very voice of Castlecombe. Its thunderous clamor beat upon their ears, filling the passage, the rooms, the galleries and courtyards, the terraces and the stately vistas of the Park; the echoes rolled and thundered, and the whole house seemed to throb, and Jeremy stood in utter bewilderment until Sally leaned across him and said:

"Is it Mickey?"

"Yes, that's Mickey," said Clive.

"Oh, glorious Mickey! Oh, well done, well done!"

Beneath the tumult other sounds were faintly audible, sounds of men running toward one another and shouting to make themselves heard, sounds of agitation and bewilderment, a sudden confusion that seemed to run through the entire house.

"He's picked the right moment!" said Clive. "We must go."

They started together down the long, narrow passage. But suddenly they stopped.

A light shone in the dark distance ahead of them, a pale small light surrounded by quivering shadows. It was moving up another stairway, and as it reached their level they saw that it was not the beam of a torch or lantern but a naked flame.

Jeremy's heart seemed to stop beating. It was the dream all over again! For a moment he was sure that he would see a rushlight carried by a man with a patch over one eye and a bandage round his head. Then he realized who it was.

The light was that of a candle, and the man who carried it no longer had a hat pulled down over his eyes. He was dark-haired and lean-faced, like Clive, and he wore a tweed jacket and a collar and tie.

They went toward him. The clanging of the bell stopped abruptly, and its echoes died slowly away, leaving a profound silence. They came together by the light of the candle, and the stranger said in a voice which Jeremy already knew:

"Clive and Sally! I thought I should find you in the end. Do you know who I am?"

"I think you're Uncle Steven," said Sally. "You recited the 'Wanderer's Song.'"

"Yes. The wanderer returned! I've been away a long

time." He bent and kissed her. "You were only two, my darling, when last we met."

He turned to Clive and took his hand for a moment.

"I'm sorry I left it till the last minute," he said in a low voice. "Who was that ringing the bell?"

"It was a friend of ours—Mickey Few."

"Mickey!" exclaimed Steven Palfrey with a laugh of astonishment. "So he's here, too! And this is Jeremy. We've already met."

"He's part of us now," Sally said.

"Of course," said Steven, as though he had known this already. "But we must hurry. Can someone give me a torch? I lost mine in the Park, and this candle was all I could find."

He took Sally's torch and turned to lead the way, but then he turned back to them.

"Do you know where to look?"

"Well, not exactly," said Clive. "But we thought—"

"You thought of the prophecy, and that this was the time! Was that it?"

"Yes."

"You believed it in spite of everyone?"

"Yes," said Clive, a little impatiently.

"It's more wonderful than you think," said Steven softly. "You've made it come true."

CHAPTER 13

the secret place

THE RINGING OF THE BELL HAD CLEARED the way for them. While the keepers ran instinctively in the direction of the sound, thinking of fire and other calamities, they were free to make their roundabout way to the very heart of the house, where the fortress tower stood frowning over the biggest of the inner courtyards, with ancient buildings on either side. It was a journey through darkness that was like a journey in a dream, or a journey into the past.

There had been a time when Castlecombe, like other great country houses, was largely self-supporting, baking its own bread, brewing its own ale, curing hams and shoeing horses, carrying out all manner of repairs, and even spinning and weaving its own cloth. The traces of these activities were still to be found in rooms and halls of which some had been put to other uses, while others now stood empty, with old equipment crumbling into dust. All this accounted in part for the size of the house, but its vast extent was far more owing to the extravagant nature of the Palfreys, who had built for the pleasure of building, according to the need or fancy of the moment, each successive generation pursuing its own ideas, and none conforming to any general plan.

Jeremy had glimpses of these traces of bygone days in the occasional flicker of the torch as they passed along passages and galleries, through rooms, and up and down stairways. They were twice diverted, once by a door that Clive could not unlock and once by sounds ahead of them which obliged them to go a longer way round; but at last they reached a tangle of rooms below the Tower House—kitchen and bakery, larders, sculleries, and still-rooms—and from here they climbed a spiral staircase to a broad corridor with shuttered windows on one side and on the other side a single large door.

Steven Palfrey put his hand on it and uttered a little exclamation as it opened.

"I was sure this one would be locked!"

"Mickey saw to it," said Clive. "I had a feeling we might want to come in here, although—"

He said no more. They entered a series of rooms with communicating doors—a sitting room, a boudoir, a huge bedroom with a dressing room beyond it.

"The grand suite," Sally murmured in Jeremy's ear. "It's where the lord and lady used to live; but Grandfather never would—he said it was too gloomy."

And so the rooms with all their furniture had remained empty through the years. The beam of the torch flickered over long window curtains and oak-paneled walls, over wardrobes and carved oak chairs and a canopy bed that in itself was the size of a small room, until finally it came to rest on the spread of paneling beside the big open fireplace. There was a tall, narrow mirror here that seemed to be part of the wall; but a handle beside it showed that it covered a door.

"Do you know what that is?" Steven asked.

"Of course," said Clive. "There's nothing secret about it. It leads to what we call the fancy-dress wardrobe, full of very old clothes. We used some of them in the pageant a few years ago."

"Before that it was the powder closet," said Sally, "in the days when they had to have somewhere separate to powder their wigs, because of the mess it made."

Their voices sounded puzzled. Steven said:

"We'll go up. Clive, will you bring a chair?"

Steven opened the door and led the way up a narrow, curved flight of wooden stairs. There was a curtain at the top, and beyond it a square, low-ceilinged, windowless place which was very small for a room but large for a wardrobe.

One could not think of it as anything but a wardrobe. It was filled to the ceiling with a rough wooden framework supporting hooks and rods from which clothes hung on hangers, pressed together, partly shrouded in newspaper and smelling strongly of moth balls. Clive switched on his torch to give more light. Jeremy saw the tarnished epaulette on an officer's tunic dating from the Crimean

War; he saw long, ceremonial robes and the silks and quilted satins of women's dresses. The three of them stayed grouped by the entrance while Steven thrust his way among all this, and Sally cried:

"But it wasn't like this at all! It was quite different. There wasn't a door with a looking glass, for one thing. We—we seemed to go through the wall. The stairs were much steeper and narrower, almost like a ladder. And there was a door at the top. And it was a little bare room with rushes on the floor and a great black beam."

Steven was looking at her, and now it was he who was puzzled.

"How did you know all that? You're thinking of something much older than the powder closet. I'll show you your beam. It's still here."

He pushed some of the clothes aside, and Jeremy now saw that a low protrusion ran across the ceiling, not black but dingy white. Steven took a chisel out of his pocket, and after working a little while wrenched away a sheet of plasterboard, bringing a shower of plaster with it. He tore off other strips of board, and then they saw a black, shallow beam more than a foot wide, with one edge slightly rounded.

Steven produced another tool from his pocket, a long, stout screw driver, and thrust it into the ceiling beside the beam, bringing down more plaster. He worked the screw driver about, and finally there was a scraping sound as he thrust back a bolt. Then he got on the chair Clive had brought, and flexing his legs pushed strongly upward. It was something of a struggle. The three watchers were holding their breath. Suddenly a section of the beam swung back, leaving a hole about two feet long and a foot wide.

"There!" said Steven, panting a little and smiling at them. "The secret exit from a secret room! But old Jeremy Palfrey had another use for it. Clive, you're nippier than I am. Go up and see what you can find."

He got down from the chair, and Clive leaped up through the hole like a rabbit going to cover. He vanished from their sight, but not for long. After a few moments his head and arm appeared as he reached down with a long object wrapped in dusty sacking. Steven took it from him and Clive vanished again without a word. They stood waiting in silence until he reappeared with another parcel, smaller and more carefully wrapped. He handed this, too, to Steven, and without a word dropped back into the room.

No one spoke. It was a grave and solemn moment. They stood in the little stuffy room lighted by the beam of modern torches, with the garments of the past hanging like ghosts in their newspaper shrouds, rustling when they were disturbed and shedding clouds of dust. Steven unwrapped the Sword, the seaman's cutlass in its leather scabbard, with its big handle and brass guard. He drew it a little way from its sheath so that they could see the heavy curved blade, and then handed it to Clive.

He unwrapped the Casket. Jeremy had a moment of disappointment. He had been looking for the bright glitter of gold, as Sally had described it; but the box was dull in color, being tarnished after so many years. He knew it, nevertheless, by the six molded legs shaped like claws, and through the dirt and tarnish he could see an elaborate, heavily chased design on its slightly curved lid.

"And here it is," said Steven with a little sigh. "Still here after three hundred years! I wonder what Spanish grandee it belonged to? What beautiful lady was it intended for? And how did old Jeremy Palfrey come by it? Perhaps it's just as well that we don't know."

He was handling the Casket with his fingers outspread. There was an intricate concealed catch. He seemed to press in several places at once, and it opened with a slight click. He raised the lid and took out a yellowed, folded sheet of parchment. The Casket was lined with sandalwood and padded satin, faded and rotting; but within this was a cluster of objects that seemed to spring to life in the light of the torches, putting forth a thousand sparkles of white and red.

Steven handed the Casket to Clive, who took it and held it for the others to see.

"Diamonds and rubies," he said softly. "Diamonds from Brazil. Treasure from the ports of the Caribbean and the secret stores of Mexico. That Spanish grandee was obviously a collector. He wanted nothing but the best. I don't know how much a king's ransom is, but I'm sure these are worth enough to ransom Castlecombe."

There was silence again. Sally was touching the glittering stones gently with one finger. Neither she nor Clive

had spoken a word, but they had gazed at each other with eyes in which there was a light of awe and wonder. Suddenly Clive said:

"But how did you find out all this? How did you know?"

He was regarding his uncle with a half-frown, as though he thought Steven had played a trick of some kind. Sally raised her head and asked:

"Did you have a dream, too?"

"A dream?" Steven glanced at her in perplexity. "No, it was nothing like that. It was simply an accident. It happened just before I left England, ten years ago."

"All that time!" cried Clive. "And you never said a word!" His face had darkened in sudden anger, but Steven smiled.

"Have you forgotten the prophecy? As a matter of fact, there were two reasons why I said nothing, and this is one of them." He held up the folded parchment he had taken from the Casket. "But it's a long story, and I think—"

He broke off. Clive, too, had stiffened. They both stood listening to certain distant sounds which Jeremy now began to hear.

"The enemy approaches!" Steven said.

"Breathing fire and slaughter!" said Clive, and he grinned.

Steven took the Casket, replaced the parchment, snapped down the lid, and handed the box to Sally.

"You must carry it," he said. "Clive and Jeremy, you must go on either side of her. And I'll be the armed escort, if you'll allow me to have the Sword."

"But what are we going to do?" asked Sally. "Oughtn't we to make a bolt for it?" She glanced at the hole in the ceiling.

"No, my dear. I think the Palfreys have done enough running. We've singed McDougal's beard very prettily. The time has come for us to meet him face to face."

Steven led the way down the stairs bearing the unsheathed Sword. Sally followed with the Casket, and Clive and Jeremy came behind. They left the hole in the ceiling as it was. It had served its purpose. It would never be used again.

The big bedroom was still dark and empty, but when they emerged into the corridor they saw a light. A dark-shirted keeper came running toward them, blowing a whistle.

"Hey!" he shouted. "Hey!"

"We want to see Mr. Mungo McDougal," Steven said.

The man seemed taken aback by the coolness of his voice, and he glanced uneasily at the naked cutlass in his hand.

"You can see 'im, all right," he said with a note of truculence. "You'll have to come to the Great Hall. But you're caught now, and don't you forget it. The place is full of people. I shouldn't try any tricks if I was you."

"We shall do whatever we feel like doing," said Steven. "At the moment we feel like talking to your boss. Lead on, fellow! We shan't run away."

He flourished the cutlass, and the man went ahead of them, glancing uncomfortably over his shoulder.

Meanwhile other men had come running in response to the whistle, so that they had an escort of four by the time they reached the courtyard. Jeremy glanced up at the fortress tower looming over them, and he saw that there was a flush of gold in the sky. The night was ended.

More men appeared, and Moggs was one of them. He came up to them with malice gleaming in his little piggy eyes.

"So they've got you!" he said viciously. "And now you're going to pay for the things you've done this night! And it's you, is it, Mr. Steven? The bad penny returned! Well, this is a poor look-out for you, sir, I'm afraid."

Steven glanced at him disdainfully without troubling to reply, but Clive said cheerfully:

"Not gone to bed yet, Moggsie? How are your poor feet?"

They passed up some steps, through a doorway, along a passage, and so into the Great Hall, where the chandelier and other lights were still burning, already beginning to look pale. McDougal was not there, but there were several more keepers, including Sam. And seated on a chair, with a man standing guard over him, was Mickey Few.

"Oh, Mickey!" Sally cried as she saw him. "So you didn't manage to get away after you'd been so splendid, ringing the bell! Oh, what a shame!"

"I went on ringing it a bit too long," said Mickey, seeming not at all downcast. "Just out of devilment, as you might say. They was buzzing round me like gnats before I could bring myself to leave off." His voice changed. "Mr. Steven, sir!" he exclaimed. "This is a sight for sore eyes!"

"We seem to have been on hand at the right moment, Mick," said Steven. "As one wanderer to another I salute you!" And he raised his cutlass.

Then McDougal appeared. He came storming in, his face contorted with fury, and he strode up to Steven.

"So you're another of them! You've been aiding and

abetting these children! You've been using firearms and fireworks to stampede the animals in the Park, causing serious damage and risking injury to my keepers. And now it seems you've been caught breaking and entering the house. Let me tell you, sir—"

But his voice trailed strangely away. His mouth fell open and he was silent. He was staring at the Sword in Steven's hand and at the Casket which Sally carried.

"Do you happen to know what these are, Mr. McDougal?" asked Steven calmly. "You look as though you did."

"He knows, all right," said Clive. "He was born here, you see."

"He was a stableboy," said Jeremy, "but he ran away."

"A stableboy!" Mickey Few was leaning forward, staring hard at McDougal. "So that's it! I'd been wondering where I'd seen you before, mate. It was a long time ago. You're Ned Hawkins, that's who you are! But as for running away—it was more like bein' thrown out, wasn't it? There was a bit of trouble, as I recollect, and—"

McDougal uttered a growl, and Steven said:

"I don't think we need rake up ancient history, Mick. It must have been a very long time ago."

"Ay," muttered Mickey. "But he can't say he wasn't treated fair. He was sent away with money in his pocket to give him a start in the world—and he seems to have made the most of it!"

"You were going to tell me something, Mr. McDougal?" Steven said.

"Yes," said McDougal. "But for a start I'll trouble the young lady to hand over that box she's got. I—"

He was reaching for it as he spoke, and Clive and Jeremy closed in on Sally to protect her, and Steven swung the cutlass so that the flat of the blade came down heavily on McDougal's wrist. He drew back with an exclamation of pain and stood glaring.

"All right!" he said. "So now we can add assault to the list of charges I'll be bringing against you. You may not know it, but I'm in legal possession of this house, and nothing in it can be taken away until the money that's owing to me has been paid. I've got the law on my side."

"Up to a point," said Steven. "There's a legal agreement. But as you very well know, Mr. McDougal, it includes an inventory—a list, hundreds of pages long, of all the things the house contains, furniture, pictures, and everything. Nothing on that list can be removed from the house until the money has been paid. But the list says nothing about a gold casket filled with precious stones. It isn't mentioned because nobody believed it to exist!"

He paused, smiling at McDougal, who was breathing heavily and rubbing his wrist. The keepers had gathered round and were listening.

"If you had found this casket, Mr. McDougal," Steven went on, "it would have been your duty as a law-abiding citizen to hand it over to the police in order that its legal ownership might be established. *And that is what we intend to do!* You can bring all kinds of charges against us, if you choose, and we shall have to answer to them; but in this particular matter the law is on our side, not on yours. When we leave this house the Casket will go with us—under police escort, if you prefer it that way. Do I understand that you've sent for the police?"

McDougal did not answer this question. He drew back a pace and spoke to the keepers.

"Listen, you men. They're helpless if they haven't got that box in their possession. It can be shoved away out of sight, and who's to prove anything? All we have to do is to take it away from them. I'll pay a hundred-pound bonus to each man."

For a moment no one answered. The men exchanged glances and then looked at Sam. He shook his head.

"We can't do that, sir. The law's the law. I reckon this is a job for the police, like the gentleman said. He asked you if you'd sent for them."

"Two hundred!" said McDougal, almost shouting the words. "Are you men crazy? Don't you know which side your bread's buttered? I'm a rich man. I can pay for what I want. Five hundred! Five hundred pounds for each man jack of you if I get that box!"

There was a little stir among the men. Five hundred pounds was a lot of money. There were some, perhaps, who would have given way. But then a sound from outside caused them all to look toward the door. A car had driven up to the house.

Sam moved quickly, before anything could be said or done. He passed through the lobby, and they heard him opening the front door. Three people entered, the first two being a police sergeant and a constable. The sergeant said:

"We heard the bell tolling. I rang up the house but no one answered the phone. I thought we'd better come along to see if there was any trouble."

Jeremy missed most of what happened during the next few minutes because the third person was Aunt Eleanor. He went to meet her, and she cried:

"Oh, Jeremy, are you all right?"

"Yes, I'm perfectly all right," said Jeremy. "Only a bit tired." He had suddenly begun to feel enormously tired.

Aunt Eleanor dropped on one knee and put her hands on his arms while she examined him.

"But what have you been doing? You're black from head to foot!"

Jeremy had had no time to notice this.

"I was being a bat," he said, and smiled at her. "I had to escape up the chimney. But that part was easy. It's only a fraction of the things that happened. I'll tell you all about it when I've had a rest."

"I've been so worried. That awful dogfight, or whatever it was! I'd have been over the wall to look for you if Steven hadn't stopped me. He wouldn't even tell me what it was all about, although he seemed to know. But your legs, Jeremy! Your knees are absolutely raw! And you've bruised your mouth. Heavens—if your parents could see you!"

"But they can't, can they?" said Jeremy happily. "And it's all over now."

She kissed him suddenly, and he surprised himself by kissing her back.

"Now you've got a dirty face, too," he said.

McDougal, Steven, and the police sergeant seemed to be having a sort of conference, while the men stood round listening. At last the sergeant said:

"Well, then, sir, it's understood that you raise no objection to this box being taken out of the house?"

"No," said McDougal. "I make no claim to it."

He spoke in a low voice, heavy and oppressed, accepting his defeat.

"Very well," said the sergeant. "And now there's the question of this—this commotion in the Park."

"That's an entirely different matter," said McDougal, speaking more sharply. "Two of my men were thrown from their horses. They might have been seriously injured."

"I wanged one of them with a catapult," said Clive. "The fireworks were my idea, too. It doesn't matter who threw them. I thought of it."

"We were all in it together," Jeremy said.

"You assaulted one of the men with a catapult, did you?" said the sergeant sternly to Clive. "Now that's serious, young man, as you very well know. If a charge is brought—"

"And what about me?" said Moggs. "I was assaulted,

too. I was dragged down to the cellar and threatened with torture if I didn't do what they said."

"That's right," said Mickey cheerfully. "I said we'd put 'im in a cage and have him eaten by rats, starting at the feet and working up, like they used to do in China. And after that I was going to pull 'is teeth out, one by one!"

Mickey was perched on the edge of his chair like a little bird, with his bowler hat tilted to one side. The idea of his torturing anyone was so absurd that everyone laughed except Moggs.

"Anyone who got hurt is entitled to full compensation," said Steven. "I can promise you there'll be no argument about that."

There was a murmur of approval from the men. The sergeant looked at McDougal and said:

"Well, it seems to be up to you, sir. Do you intend to prefer charges?"

There was a dead silence while they waited for McDougal to speak. A little flicker passed over his face and he shook his head.

"No. This was a private matter. They fought in their way, and I fought in mine. I never thought it possible that— But they've won, and that's all there is about it. I don't bring charges against children."

"Good old Mungo!" murmured Clive, and McDougal glared at him.

And then the meeting broke up. Jeremy found when they got outside that Aunt Eleanor's car was parked behind the police car. She had sat up all night waiting for news of him, and when she heard the tolling of the bell she had driven straight to the police station. Jeremy gathered this in a dreamy sort of way. Aunt Eleanor had one arm round him and the other arm round Sally. They both got into the back of her car while Clive and Steven and Mickey got into the police car, taking the Casket.

They went down the drive and along the avenue leading to the main gate. Deer and antelope bounded under the trees as they approached, but Jeremy was too sleepy to notice. The sun had risen, the air was filled with light and warmth and the song of birds, and Sally said:

"It's going to be another lovely day but I don't suppose we shall see much of it. Too sleepy! And it won't be like yesterday, will it? Or last night. Nothing will ever be quite so wonderful again." She gave a great yawn and her head drooped against Jeremy's shoulder. "So we've saved Castlecombe. Well, we knew we would. But it's a queer thing. When the battle's over, and you've won, you think you'll be madly excited, but you aren't; you just want to sleep for a hundred years."

CHAPTER 14

the long and the short of it

BUT OF COURSE IT WAS STILL NOT QUITE over. There were a great many things to be done, and there was a story to be told.

With the things that had to be done Jeremy was not concerned. Steven and Clive went straight up to London to attend to legal matters which had to be settled in a great hurry, in order that the diamonds might be sold and the money repaid to McDougal before the time expired. Sally spent twenty-four hours in Aunt Eleanor's cottage, sleeping most of the time, and then a car came for her and she, too, was borne off to London. But they were all planning to come back to Castlecombe at the end of a week.

During this time Jeremy and Aunt Eleanor lived quietly, doing the sort of things Jeremy's parents would have expected them to do, including paying two visits to the fair at Reddicombe. Nothing special happened except that Jeremy heard two important pieces of news.

The first was sad. The Old Earl—Steven's father and Clive and Sally's grandfather—was dead. He had died in a hospital in Nairobi on the very day Jeremy had got into the Park. The papers said that he had been ill for some time, although this was something that Clive and Sally had certainly not known.

The Old Earl had had three sons, of whom Clive's father, Nigel, had been the eldest. The second son, Tristram, lived in France; and the third was Steven. But since Clive was the only son of the eldest son, he was now the Earl of Castlecombe.

It took a bit of getting used to. Clive! Jeremy had never imagined himself being friendly with an earl.

"Well, I'm sure of one thing," he said after thinking it over. "It won't change him. He'll be just the same."

"So I should hope!" said Aunt Eleanor. She looked at Jeremy for a moment and then said: "Do you remember my telling you that our family used to live near here?"

"Yes."

"As a matter of fact, we're connected with the Palfreys. My great-grandmother, and your great-great-grandmother, was one of the daughters."

Jeremy gave a gasp.

"What! Do you mean to say I'm a cousin of—"

"Scarcely a cousin. A distant relation, that's all."

"But why didn't you tell me?"

"For one thing, because I didn't want you to get too interested in the Park. I didn't want you to go climbing over the wall and getting into trouble when you were supposed to be recovering from measles. In any case, your father might have told you at any time, if he'd thought of it. It's interesting, you see, but not really so important. You had seven other great-great-grandmothers, don't forget. We're all related to all kinds of people, if we go back far enough. We're all a part of history, as I said to you once before."

"Yes," said Jeremy. "But still—"

"People are apt to be silly and snobbish about titles," said Aunt Eleanor. "They're not much more than an ornament in these days. Breeding is what really matters, and you don't need any kind of title to have that."

But to Jeremy it was a revelation. It seemed to him to account for all kinds of things that he had been unable to explain—the feeling he had had, for instance, when he had first heard the trumpet call. He was so filled with amazement that it was a long time before he could say anything, but at length he asked:

"Do you think that's why my name is Jeremy?"

"It may be," said Aunt Eleanor. "It's a name that runs in the Palfrey family, I believe."

Another thought occurred to him.

"And is that why you came to live in these parts?"

"Well, perhaps—a little," said Aunt Eleanor, and she smiled.

She was keeping a secret, as Jeremy well knew; and he did not need to be told that it was something to do with Steven. There was a great change in Aunt Eleanor. She looked young and glowing with happiness. She looked different in other ways, too. She had had something done to her hair, and she had bought some new clothes. Jeremy remembered his mother saying that she would be very pretty if only she would take more trouble with herself. Well, she was taking trouble now—and Mother was quite right!

So the week passed, and a day came when Jeremy was sent out to pick every strawberry he could find in preparation for a tea party. The day was fine and warm, although there had been rain during the week. Jeremy had just finished putting up garden chairs on the lawn behind the cottage when he heard the car drive up, and he ran round to the front to meet it.

He scarcely noticed Steven. Clive and Sally were looking very different from when he had last seen them. They were clean, for one thing. Sally was wearing a gay-colored frock, and Clive had on what looked like a new sports jacket. But his grin was the same as ever, and there was really nothing about him to lead one to suppose that this was the Earl of Castlecombe.

Jeremy was bursting with his news.

"Do you know what?" he said. "I'm a relation of yours!"

He told them about it and Sally cried:

"Oh, Jeremy, how lovely! Of course, that explains everything."

"Not that it makes any odds," said Clive. "We'd made you an adopted cousin anyway."

"Which means you can come and stay at Castlecombe

whenever you like," said Sally. "There'll always be a room for you."

"In fact, about forty," said Clive. "You can have the grand suite, if you like, and practice roller skating in the bedroom—it's big enough. By the way, we've brought you a present."

He thrust a small packet into Jeremy's hand, looking a little shy as he did so. It was a wrist watch, a very good one, with Jeremy's name on the back—just about the best present he had ever had. It so took his breath away that he could scarcely thank them.

Clive was also carrying a very bulky parcel, but this was for the last member of the party, who had not yet arrived. Steven had gone off somewhere with Aunt Eleanor, so they wandered round the garden, all talking at once, and Jeremy learned about the things that had been happening in London. Everything was settled. The stones had been sold, all except a few which were to make earrings and a pendant for Sally when she was older, and the money had been paid back, and Castlecombe was safe, and McDougal was at that moment packing his traps to leave; but as he had not yet gone they had thought it better to have the tea party on Aunt Eleanor's lawn.

Then Mickey drove up in his van, bringing Prince with him, although Jeremy never found time to ask how this had come about. Sally hugged them both, and while Clive was examining Prince to make sure that his wounds were healing properly Mickey examined the contents of his parcel. It was an accordion, black with ivory keys, about twice the size of his old one. He ran his fingers over the keys, looking rather as Jeremy had done when he strapped on the wrist watch.

"I shall have to make up a special song for it," he said. "It'll have to be a good 'un."

"About fireworks, or ringing the great bell of Castlecombe," said Sally.

"Or just about being young," Mickey said.

Emma came out at that moment, pushing a tea wagon and calling: "Miss Eleanor, where have you got to? Everything's all ready." And after a minute or two Aunt Eleanor and Steven appeared from somewhere or other, Aunt Eleanor looking rather pink, and they all had tea.

Emma had made enough cakes and sandwiches for a dozen people, and it was lucky that they had Prince to help them out. He lay at Sally's feet, accepting what was offered but never asking, while Aunt Eleanor's terrier, Buster, crouched under Aunt Eleanor's chair, never taking his eyes off him.

The tea vanished, and presently the talk and laughter died down and there was a silence.

"Uncle Steven," said Sally, "it's time you told us!"

"Told you?" said Steven.

"You're not to go on being tiresome! You've been putting us off for days. We want to know why you went away, and why you didn't write to anyone, and how you managed to come back at the crucial moment, and how you knew about the hiding place and—everything."

"And why you never told anyone before," said Clive.

"Very well," Steven said.

He got out a pipe and started to fill it while he looked at Clive.

"Didn't you know that the powder closet was originally a secret room?"

Clive shook his head.

"I suppose nobody thought of telling you. That's what happens in an old place like Castlecombe. Things get covered up. They change their shape, and people forget. Well, anyway, that's what it was. I can't tell you when it was built. There have been plenty of times when the Palfreys may have wanted to hide fugitives in Castlecombe. But a time came, later, when there was no need for a secret room; and when powdered wigs came into fashion someone had the idea of making it into a powder closet. So they did away with the secret entrance—a sliding panel, or whatever it was—and put in an ordinary door. And they did up the room, and very likely they widened the stairs so that a lady in panniered skirts could get up and down more easily. They made it all look quite different. But in the beginning, you see, it must have been pretty much like the room you imagined."

"The room we dreamed of," said Sally in a low voice. "Both of us together. And that's something you can't ever explain."

"No," said Steven. "No one can explain that."

"The powder closet . . ." muttered Clive. "And we thought we knew all about it. But it was a queer place for a secret room—off the grand suite."

"A handy place in some ways. When they were hiding someone, my lord or my lady could stay in bed pretending to be ill, and have meals brought up without any questions being asked. Servants' gossip must always have been one of the dangers. But let me go on with the story.

"During the last winter of the war I came home on leave. It was a terrible time, terribly hard and sad. The last big battle was being fought, in the Ardennes. My brother Nigel had been killed a few months before, and I'd been wounded, not very badly. I turned up at Castlecombe just after Christmas, and found no one there but Father. I don't know where you children were—living somewhere near London, I think, with your mother. Clive must have been about four then, and Sally was still a baby. There was only Father, with no one but the Moggses and a few servants to keep him company.

"I can't tell you how dreary the house was. The weather was awful, snow and sleet and bitterly cold, so that there was nothing much to be done out-of-doors. And Father had had one of his sudden ideas and was pottering about the house, opening wardrobes and closets and fishing out old clothes, some of which had been stowed away for generations.

"He talked about selling them, but I told him not to be absurd—the Palfreys weren't old-clothes dealers! In any case, although some of them were very old and interesting, they weren't worth anything in terms of money. I said that the thing to do was to get the best of them cleaned up, and later he might present them to a museum.

In the meantime we needed somewhere safe to put them, and I thought of the powder closet. It's hard by the chimney, as you know, and there's a furnace in the basement. At least they would be kept fairly dry.

"I said I'd rig up a framework for the hangers and turn the closet into a wardrobe. I was glad to have something to do. So I started to clean it out. You can imagine what it was like—knee-deep in dust and cobwebs, with the plaster bellying down from the ceiling where the laths had rotted. It all had to be stripped away, and it turned out that there was another ceiling above it, which was rotten, too. The end of it was that I pulled down about a dozen barrowloads of plaster and rotting wood, and entirely uncovered the beam, which had been only just visible before. And then I found that there was something queer about it. There was a sort of bolt, made of bronze, high up on one side. The middle section was pivoted on the end sections, so that it could be made to swing back when the bolt was drawn. I'll show you when we get back to the house. It was all very stiff and difficult, but it still worked. Some old craftsman had done a wonderful job.

"I guessed at once that it was a secret way out of the secret room. There was probably some way of getting onto the roof, or perhaps into a chimney. But I never found out about that. I saw two objects wrapped in cloth resting on a plank stretched across the timbers, close to the beam. They were half buried in dust. I might easily have overlooked them. I had no idea what they were.

"I wasn't thinking of the prophecy at all. I had never taken it very seriously. I thought that if old Jeremy Palfrey had really left something behind, someone must have found it long ago and made off with it without saying anything. It could have been a servant or a man doing repairs, or even one of the family—not all our ancestors were strictly honest, as we know. I didn't realize until I had got the casket open, which was a tricky job because the mechanism of the catch was rusty and clogged with dust. But then I knew. And after thinking it over I decided what I must do."

Steven paused, and they all waited. Mickey said:

"One thing you haven't mentioned is that I helped you with that room."

"I was just going to. Yes, Mickey was there. He'd called two days before this happened, to see if there were any jobs to be done. He was a godsend. I'd never have managed without him. But as luck would have it he wasn't in the room when I found the things. I didn't tell him. I put them in a cupboard for a few days, and then, when we'd started on the new ceiling, I put them back where they came from. You never suspected anything, did you, Mick?"

"Of course not. I'd never even heard of 'em then. Matter of fact," said Mickey, "that's the very last place in the whole house where I'd have thought of looking, seeing that you'd been up there."

"Yes," said Steven. "And by the time we'd repaired the ceiling and covered the beam with plasterboard, which

I did deliberately, the Casket and the Sword were more securely hidden than they had ever been."

"But I don't see it!" cried Clive. "Why should you have hidden them again and never said a word?"

"For two reasons. I'll tell you later. Let me first finish my own story.

"My leave was nearly up, but before I left home a thing happened which I don't like to remember. I had a bad quarrel with my father.

"It was about money. The war was ending, and I was wondering what I was going to do when I came out of the Army. I was only a younger son—I had to earn my living. A friend of mine had offered me a partnership in his business if I could find a few thousand pounds. I asked Father if he would put up the money, and he refused.

"Father had never talked to me about money matters, or to anyone. Of course I knew that the family was nothing like as rich as it had been. Building the wall alone had cost a fortune. But I didn't dream that he was already in serious trouble—so hard up, in fact, that he had even thought of trying to raise a little money by selling those old clothes! The thought never occurred to me, and when he said he couldn't afford to help me I thought he was just being mean.

"I never asked again. I never said anything at all, but I felt rather bitter, and Father and I were never really friendly after that. And when I came out of the Army I was offered a job in North Africa by a British firm. It wasn't much of a job, but it looked as though it might improve, and as it happened I had a rather special reason then for grabbing the first job I could get."

Steven hesitated, smiling a little.

"I'd met someone, you see—a girl who was learning to paint. I wanted to ask her to marry me, but I was too poor at the time. I hoped that if the job turned out well I might come back and do so in a year or two."

"If you'd had the sense to say something you'd have found that she didn't care twopence about the money," said Aunt Eleanor, while a flush spread over her face. "She'd have gone with you to North Africa or anywhere else."

"Yes," said Steven, "I know that now. . . . But in any case, the job didn't work out. The firm when bankrupt about a year later. Things went badly for me for a long time. I drifted in and out of jobs, and in and out of places. In short, I became one of the roving Palfreys, without ever having meant to. I began to feel that I was a failure. I stopped writing to my friends and family, and so their letters stopped coming and I didn't know anything about what was happening at home."

"I wrote two letters that you didn't answer," Aunt Eleanor said.

"They never reached me. I was moving about. I thought you'd forgotten me, my dear, and I couldn't blame you for that. It was not until about two years ago that my luck began to change. I'd reached South America by then. I got a job on a big cattle ranch in Argentina, and after a year I was made manager. I began to do well, in fact, and I was just planning a trip to England when a strange thing happened. I was spending a few days in Buenos Aires. A man came up to me in the hotel and asked if I was the Honorable Steven Palfrey, third son of the Earl of Castlecombe. I said I was, and when I'd produced documents to prove it he gave me an envelope. He was a private inquiry agent employed by the family lawyers in London to find me.

"The envelope contained two letters, and one of them was from my father. He wrote to beg me, wherever I might be, to come home and take care of Clive and Sally. And he said—" Steven broke off and looked at Clive. "I think this letter must have been written at about the time when he told you the real state of affairs at Castlecombe, or perhaps a little earlier. Were you near a town at the time?"

"We were stopping just outside Nairobi," said Clive.

"Did Father go to see a doctor?"

"Not that I know of. He saw a lot of people, and we thought it was about business. He didn't say anything about a doctor."

"He didn't tell you. He was seriously ill, you see, and he knew he hadn't much longer to live. I think it was knowing this that made him—well, realize things. He told me what a mess everything was in, and then he talked about you two again. He said, 'I hope they won't come to hate my memory, although I deserve that they should. By my folly and extravagance I have squandered Clive's inheritance and betrayed Castlecombe.' "

There was a long silence. Clive gave a sudden violent shake of his head and made a movement with his clenched fist as though he wanted to hit someone. He said in a low voice:

"Grandfather was good to us *always.* I don't care what he did!"

Sally said nothing at all. She was sitting very straight, looking steadily at Steven, while tears rolled down her cheeks.

"There was a letter from the lawyers as well," Steven went on. "It told me a bit more about the position—details of the loan from McDougal, and so on. This was just three weeks ago. I can't tell you what a shock it was to me. I blamed myself bitterly for having gone off, as I had done, and not kept in touch with the family. I should have liked to go to my father, but there was no time. I could only send him a cable telling him not to worry about losing Castlecombe. I had to wait more than a week for an air passage, and then I flew to London and went straight to the lawyers' offices.

"I wanted to see Clive and Sally, but although they were back in England no one could tell me exactly where they were. I rang up various relations, who all said they were staying with someone else. It was rather puzzling."

Clive grinned faintly at this, and even Sally smiled through her tears.

"But I must admit I didn't try very hard to track them down. The first thing was Castlecombe. I'd thought that all I should have to do was to walk into the house, make a hole in the ceiling of the closet and get the Casket, and that would be that. But I found that it wasn't going to be nearly so easy. There were legal complications. McDougal was in possession, and his men had strict orders to admit no one. There was simply no time to get the thing done in a proper legal way. The only way was to break in. That would be burglary, of course. On the other hand, once I'd actually got the Casket, McDougal would have no legal right to take it away from me, because it didn't come under the agreement. It was one of those cases where, quite literally, possession is nine points of the law.

"So I came to Castlecombe. I drove down in a hired car on the day my father died, the day Jeremy got under the wall, the day McDougal turned up, the day everything happened. I don't suppose any of us will forget that day and night as long as we live. Certainly I shan't.

"Because a miracle happened. I didn't intend to try to get in until after dark, but during the afternoon I walked round looking at the wall and wondering where would be the best place to climb over. I was very unhappy, to tell you the truth. I didn't know how many people McDougal had guarding the place, or what I should find when I got inside. It all looked pretty difficult. And then I saw a lady sitting at an easel painting a picture. I'd been thinking a good deal about a girl I used to know who studied painting. I went to look, never dreaming that it would be the same one. . . . But it was really a double miracle, because it turned out that she'd never married anyone else!"

"Too busy painting," said Aunt Eleanor. "Nothing to do with you!" Then she smiled at him. "Well, I felt sure you'd come back to Castlecombe sooner or later, like the Palfreys nearly always do."

They sat looking at each other as though they had forgotten where they were, until at last Clive said tactfully:

"You can hold hands if you like. We don't mind. But go on with the story."

Steven laughed and took Aunt Eleanor's hand and went on.

"There isn't much more. I heard about Jeremy, and about trumpet calls and a boy who sent a message tied to an arrow. And then, of course, I knew where Clive and Sally had got to. It was wonderful to know, although I could still only guess at what you were doing. I thought that possibly you'd found out where the Casket and the Sword were hidden. Some old letter or document might have come to light.

"Well, it seemed best to wait, hoping Jeremy would come back; and when it began to grow dark Nell and I went down to that hillock. I kept in the shadow, for one thing because I was carrying a stepladder, all ready to get over the wall. Jeremy called out and then the arrow came, and we knew that one of you must be with him. I was just going to call and tell you who I was when the fight started between Prince and the boar, and Nell was scared half out of her wits."

"Petrified!" said Aunt Eleanor. "I thought Jeremy was being murdered!"

"And by the time I'd got across the river with my ladder I heard a police whistle blowing in the distance, and then the sound of horses. I had to wait. The end of it was that I carried the ladder some distance and got over the wall at a place where things were quieter.

"And then I scarcely knew what to do. I'd no idea how to find you. I heard a trumpet call in the distance, and presently I heard the baying of bloodhounds. A lot seemed to be going on, and I decided to make for the Stooping Lady and have a look round when the moon rose. I was just starting to climb up when I heard someone move."

"I slipped," said Jeremy.

"Yes. I hadn't seen anything. It could have been any one of you; but it was just as likely to be a keeper, posted there on watch. So I recited the 'Wanderer's Song,' and then Jeremy told me the most important thing—that you were planning to break into the house that night.

"You know the rest. Thanks to the confusion in the Park, I managed in the end to get into the house—not by the same way as Clive, of course. I had quite a job. The fact is, I came to Castlecombe without realizing what I was up against. I could never have beaten all those keepers single-handed. If it hadn't been for what the rest of you did, I don't think I should ever have got into the house at all."

"Sal and Jeremy were the real ones," Clive said. "They made it easy for Mickey and me."

"I think it was all of you," said Steven. "It happened because you believed in something that most people were too clever to believe in; because you were young enough to believe in something strange and old. . . . And that's the end of my story, except for the thing I have still to tell you. I still have to explain why I said nothing when I first found the Casket and the Sword."

"Yes," said Clive.

Steven got an envelope out of his pocket and took from it the folded sheet of parchment that had been in the Casket.

"This is one reason," he said, and spread it out for them to see.

Two messages were written on the parchment, the first in faded brown ink, and in a handwriting with many flourishes which was hard to decipher. He read it to them.

" 'Found by me, Nicholas Palfrey, on this Fourth day of March, in the Year of Our Lord, Seventeen Hundred and Five. And by me restored to its hiding place that in the fullness of Time the Prophecy may be fulfilled, since by God's Grace our Family continues prosperous and in no present need of Succor. With a Prayer for the Safety of this House.' "

The second message was written in blue ink.

" 'Found also by me, Steven Palfrey, on the 7th of January, 1945, and again restored to its hiding place, for the same reason and with the same prayer.' "

Clive had uttered a gasp as he heard the first message.

"So they'd been found before!"

"Yes," said Steven. "At the time when powdered wigs were becoming fashionable—do you see? Nicholas Palfrey was the eldest son, but he never succeeded to the title. He was killed three years later, fighting under Marlborough. He was a man who believed in prophecies, and in respecting the last wishes of the dying, so he put them back again and said nothing. I think that's how prophecies always work. They don't come true by magic. They come true for reasons, and because men have faith. When I found the Casket we were a lot less prosperous than we had been in Nicholas' day, but we still weren't threatened by any immediate disaster—at least, not so far as I knew. After seeing what he had written, what could I do, except what he had done?"

"But you said there was another reason," said Clive.

"And so there was. It's not an easy one to talk about." Steven was silent for a moment while he looked at Clive. "This was a family secret," he said. "It could only be told to a member of the family, if I told anyone at all; and the proper person to tell was the head of the family, my father. Clive, have you thought what would have been likely to happen if I had told him? You know what Father was, his head teeming with huge, extravagant ideas. How long would it have been, do you think, before he sold those diamonds? And how long would the money have lasted?"

Clive stared at him, and at last slowly nodded his head with a glum little smile.

"I'm afraid you're right," he said. "Grandfather would have blown the lot."

"And then there would have been nothing to save Castlecombe."

"Darling Grandfather!" said Sally, and again there were tears in her eyes. "We shall always love him better than anyone. But he *was* a woolgatherer. We've got to admit that."

"He belonged to a world quite different from ours," said Steven. "He was the last of the old Palfreys. They only knew how to be rich. They knew all about spending money, and they spent it in wonderful ways. The Park's a wonderful place, and so is the house, in its huge, untidy fashion. But they'd no notion of saving money, and still less of earning it. Think of that ruinous wall! And think of Father with his old clothes and his notion of finding a diamond mine, as though they grew on trees! That's why I felt I dared not tell him.

"I badly wanted to tell someone. I'd have told your father, if he'd been still alive—Nigel had his head screwed on the right way. But I wasn't so sure of Tristram. In the end all I did was to leave a letter with the lawyers, to be opened in the event of my death. So of course it never was opened. But you see I really thought that if any danger threatened Castlecombe I should be bound to know about it. I didn't foresee the things that were going to happen to me. I'm making no excuses. All that is something that I bitterly regret."

And now it seemed that everything had been told. Jeremy, who had scarcely spoken a word, sat thinking the story over, and thinking how much there was to think about. After a time Clive said:

"We Palfreys are a strange lot, aren't we? A pretty silly lot in some ways, and there's no denying it. It makes you wonder why anyone puts up with us."

He glanced at Mickey as he spoke, perhaps because Mickey was the only one who was not connected with the Palfreys, except by friendship.

"I reckon you've got your share of human nature," Mickey said cheerfully. "Good and bad, like the rest of us. But you're bigger, like—on account of having been born to it, you see."

At this moment they heard a car pull up outside.

The caller was McDougal, and the unexpectedness of his arrival took their breath away. He came stamping across the lawn toward them, with a cigar between his fingers.

"Don't get up," he said. "I'm on my way to London. I looked in to tell you that I've cleared all my stuff out of the house. You can go back whenever you like."

"Thank you, Mr. McDougal," Steven said.

"There's one other thing," said McDougal, and looked at all of them with a sort of glare. "You beat me, and that's the end of that. No hard feelings. But I still want Castlecombe. I'm ready to buy the place. I'm a rich man. I won't haggle over the price."

This again silenced them. Steven glanced at Clive and then shook his head.

"I'm sorry," he said. "Castlecombe isn't for sale."

"That's what I thought you'd say," said McDougal angrily. "You'll never learn, will you? I'll warrant you haven't got much money left, after settling with me! How long do you think you can keep that great place going? You've had a windfall, mister; that's the long and the short of it. You've saved your bacon by a bit of luck. You can't expect it to happen again."

"You might put it even more harshly," said Steven quietly, "and say that we've saved our bacon because one of our ancestors was a pirate, and we managed to find his loot. That's the long and the short of it! It's nothing to be proud of, and we know very well it won't happen again. From now on we've got to make Castlecombe earn its living. We quite realize that."

"Ah," said McDougal, and looked at him with a sudden interest. "And how do you reckon to go about it?"

"Clive and I have been talking things over," said Steven. "We think the Park should be used for breeding animals, instead of just collecting them. Cattle, for instance—pedigree bulls for sale to the Argentine, where I have a good many friends. It would have to be done on a big scale, of course, and we should have to make big changes. We should have to get rid of a lot of the woods, for one thing, to make more grassland and to make room for growing feed. We should need special buildings. It's a large undertaking."

"It would call for a lot of money," said McDougal. "More than you reckon, probably, and certainly more than you've got."

"That's true. We should have to borrow—float a company, or something." Steven seemed a little vague. "Well, there are ways of doing these things."

"Ay," said McDougal. "There are ways. There are good ways and silly ways, and from what I know of you Palfreys you'd find a silly one!" He blew a cloud of smoke and watched it for a moment, and then his shrewd eyes returned to Steven. "Listen, Mr. Palfrey. There might be something in this idea of yours. But you'd need a businessman to look after the business end. Why not let me handle it for you? You bring me a working proposition, and I'll float your company for you and see you get all the money you want."

For the third time they were all silent with astonishment.

"And take a share of the profits, Mr. McDougal?" Steven asked.

"Naturally," snapped McDougal. "I'm a businessman." But then his voice changed. "It wouldn't be for the sake of the profits. I was born in Castlecombe, don't forget. I'd like to have a hand in anything you might be doing with the place."

He seemed to be almost pleading with them, and again Steven and Clive exchanged glances.

"There's one thing, Mr. McDougal," said Clive, leaning forward in his chair. "You wouldn't try to boss us about, would you? We don't like that."

"Wait a minute!" growled McDougal. "Who d'you think you're talking to, young fellow? A lad your age . . ." But the corners of his mouth were twitching. "No," he said. "You'd run your own concern in your own way, without any interference from me. That's understood. I'd simply keep an eye on the finances and try to stop you going bankrupt. I'm not saying, mind you, that I wouldn't try to teach you a little sense!"

"Perhaps there are some things we can teach you, Mr. McDougal," said Sally. "I'll teach you to play the trumpet, if you like."

At this McDougal laughed. They all laughed, and after a final glance at Clive, Steven said:

"All right, Mr. McDougal, that's a bargain. We'll work out a plan, and then we'll come and talk to you about it."

"Good," said McDougal. "You know where to find me. Well, I'll be off now. I'm a busy man."

He turned to go, but Clive stopped him.

"Mr. McDougal, what are you going to do with those bloodhounds?"

"Do with 'em? Why, get rid of 'em, I suppose."

"Will you sell them to us?"

"What do you want them for?"

"Because they're lovely dogs," said Sally. "They're one of the gentlest of all breeds."

"There you go!" growled McDougal. "Chucking your money about, first chance you get! I'll make you a present of 'em. And now I'm going. Good-by. Good-by."

He went off, and they sat listening in silence until they heard the big car drive away.

"Well!" said Aunt Eleanor. "I think that's the most

extraordinary thing I ever heard of! You've been fighting that man tooth and nail, and now suddenly you're all friends and going into business together!"

"Why not?" said Steven. "He loves Castlecombe, in his own way. And it's an old story, my dear—the battle of the old against the new, and in the end they come to terms and work together. These things have been happening in England for a thousand years."

Then they saw that Mickey had got to his feet.

"It's time for me to be going, too," he said, smiling at them. "It's very nice here, but I'm like Mr. McDougal —I'm a busy man. I ought to have been in Exeter a week ago."

"Oh, Mickey!" cried Sally. "Why do you have to go away at all? Why can't you stay with us in Castlecombe? There'll be millions of jobs to do."

"I'll be back to attend to some of 'em," said Mickey. "Don't you fret. But it doesn't suit me to stay too long in one place, my dear. It isn't in my nature. You have your roving Palfreys, and I'm one of the roving Fews—the fewer the better, I dare say, if you'll pardon the joke. I've even got a song about it, like your 'Wanderer's Song.' Only I call mine the 'Wonderer's Song.' I'll sing it to you with my new instrument, and then I'll go."

He played a few notes on the splendid accordion, and then he sang:

"The plowman has to follow the plow,
The sailor follows the sea;

But I can only follow my nose
And that's the trouble with me.
Yes, that's the trouble with me, my dears,
Wherever I chance to be;
It seems I've got to follow my nose,
And where it leads me is where I goes;
And I wonder what lies beyond the hill
And after I've seen it I wonder still—
And that's the trouble with me
My dearies,
That's the trouble with me.

"There's some raise crops of fruit and corn
And some a family;
But all I raise is a cloud of dust
And that's the trouble with me.
Nothing to show but a cloud of dust,
And I reckon it's just because I must
Go traveling on without fixed abode,
And naught to reap where there's naught been sowed—
And that's the trouble with me
My dearies,
That's the trouble with me.

"There's some knows what and some knows why
And some knows where they be;
But all I know is the windy sky
And that's the trouble with me.
It's been the trouble my whole life long
And that's the reason I sing this song:
For fish must swim and birds must fly

And men must wonder until they die;
But still it's better to laugh than cry
And you'll not change me although you try—

"So you might as well let me be
You see?
Because that's the trouble with me, my dearies,
That's the trouble with me!"

When he had finished Mickey made a sweeping bow, taking off his bowler hat to do so, and Jeremy was amazed to discover that he was almost completely bald, which is why he always wore his hat.

They went with him to the front gate and watched him trundle away in his old van. Then they all talked at once, arranging for Aunt Eleanor and Jeremy to come and spend the whole of the next day at Castlecombe, so that they could see what it was really like. They talked about tomorrow and tomorrow and tomorrow. The tea party, like the battle, was over; and it had ended in the best way possible—with a song.

ABOUT THE AUTHOR

"Norman Dale" is the pseudonym of Norman Denny, who has written several novels, translated a number of books from French and German (including five novels and two volumes of children's stories by Marcel Aymé, THE WONDERFUL FARM and THE MAGIC PICTURES), and acted for many years as literary adviser to a well-known English publishing house. Mr. Denny was born in Kent, England, and started his literary career at the age of twelve, as editor of a school magazine. He grew up in England, but lived for two years in Mexico City, where his father was a mining engineer. Mr. Denny says that when he decided it might be a good idea to write down the stories he had been telling to his elder son, he invented Norman Dale to cover his confusion and his doubts about his ability to write for children. After ten years, though, Norman Dale's books are still successful, and have been translated into eight different languages. Mr. Denny writes: "It is hard to say whether Denny or Dale is now the senior partner. They continue to live separate lives, Denny being somewhat involved in the literary world, whereas Norman Dale stays buried in the country, writes his own kind of book, helps with the farm (under Mrs. Denny's orders) and looks after a few hives of bees (single-handed because he can't get anyone to help him)." The people that Mr. Denny can't get to help him include his wife, his two sons aged nineteen and fourteen, and his five-year-old daughter.